AN UNTAMED LYNX

IDLEWYLD MATES BOOK TWO

RENEE HEWETT

Acknowledgments

Thanks a million to Alexa and Mandy for all the pep talks and cheerleading—I wouldn't have gotten to the finish line without you! Thank you, Mandy, Bonnie, Julienne, and Alexa, for the writing sprints... again, this book wouldn't be written without them!

Thank you to Dar Albert for the cover and A. Gregory for the edits!

And thank you to the readers for giving this book a chance.

Please consider writing a review once you finish the book. Reviews help new readers find the book, but they also help me know what you want in future books.

-Renee

PROLOGUE

Esme Baer approached the Cavalli's large estate. Though imposing, the large structure represented the strength and power of Oren Cavalli himself. It gave her hope for the small bobcat kitten in her arms.

The poor thing was exhausted, and while he couldn't tell her what had happened, Esme just *knew* things.

Like where to bring the little traumatized shifter.

"Esme! We weren't expecting you!" Anaya Cavalli exclaimed with a beaming smile when one of the guards ushered Esme into the den. "What is that you have there?"

Esme looked at the beautiful woman gravely.

"I'd love to chat with you, Anaya, but I think Oren needs to know about our friend here."

Anaya's features went from surprised to understanding before she rushed toward her husband's office. He returned with her a moment later, his dark Italian features contrasting her lighter skin, blonde hair, and blue eyes.

Oren took one look at the little cat, and his serious mien snapped to attention. "How did you find him?"

"You know me. Always at the right place at the right time," Esme replied. With her reputation, she didn't need to elaborate.

Oren nodded and waved forward one of his guards. "Take this little fella up to the nursery and ask the nanny to give him lots of blankets and whatever else to make him comfortable."

The guard took the cat from Esme and left, giving them the privacy to speak openly.

"I'd heard about the shooting and the missing boy right before I found him," Esme explained. The city of Idlewyld had a reputation for violence, though Oren led an organization that did its best to thwart it.

Oren and his wife exchanged a loaded glance. "Someone is trying to prove something for the

Santibanez clan. Rolling his bones, as some used to say."

Esme shuddered at Oren's words. His jargon for committing murder to prove loyalty to a specific group was chilling, yet Esme knew it happened regularly in places like Idlewyld. More than anyone cared to admit.

Anaya gasped, horrified. "They shot the boy's parents right in front of him?"

Oren nodded. "It's their way."

"He's been in bobcat form since I found him," Esme explained. "I don't know how much he understands about what is going on around him, but something definitely drew him to me. He let me pick him up and burrowed right in my arms."

"How old is this boy?" Anaya asked.

"Ten," Oren answered. The single word was all the explanation needed.

Most shifters didn't experience their first shift until their teen years, but a traumatic event could force one. Especially when it saved their life.

Anaya's eyes lined with tears as she turned toward her husband. "Is he ours to take care of now?"

Esme waited for the answer, knowing that if Oren said yes, Anaya would instantly take to the child as if he were her own, despite having her own large brood. However, Esme didn't feel this was the kitten's final home.

Oren sighed, clearly not about to turn the kid away. "An enemy of my enemy..."

"Is our new child?" Anaya finished.

"It's too dangerous to keep him here." Oren shook his head. He took a deep, steadying breath, pursing his lips in thought. With a resigned cough, he faced Esme. "Thank you for bringing him here. You did the right thing. We'll take it from here."

Lucky for them, Esme always had an idea up her stylish sleeve. "If I may... I have an idea..."

CHAPTER

ONE

Kat rushed around the pediatric wing, doing a million little things. In a flurry of motion, she answered the nurse station's ringing phone, paged a doctor for a consult, emailed the chief of staff another plea for more supplies, and gave a nervous gentleman the right direction to his daughter's room. Kat glared at her slacking coworkers, who were pros at not doing their jobs.

"Watch out, Hurricane Kat coming through," one of the nurses grumbled as Kat organized a pile of patient files precariously perched on the desk

"Well, someone has to keep this place running," she shot back.

"It runs just fine."

The *it ran fine before you got here* was left unsaid, so Kat held her tongue.

Since taking the position at Idlewyld General a year ago, Kat kept busy. While a few well-meaning coworkers suggested that she was too intense, Kat couldn't dial it back. Sometimes she felt like a snowball crashing down a mountain, getting bigger and more dangerous with each roll.

Her coworkers had welcomed her at first, but they distanced themselves as the months went on, alienated by her competence and her standard of care. Kat dealt with it. Her priority was the children—their patients—not making friends.

At least, that's what she told herself. She was all about partying with friends in her younger years, but she grew up. Now was the time to be serious, to do the best job she could do. No matter how unlikeable it made her to the others.

"Someone here to see you," another nurse said, walking by. "She's in waiting room A."

The sitting room was cozy and private, perfect for personal and sensitive conversation.

The nurse was already gone before Kat could ask who the visitor was. "I'm taking my ten," Kat announced to her colleagues before she headed to the room.

To her shock, it wasn't a patient waiting but a familiar friendly face.

"Esme!" Kat entered and embraced the elegant woman, careful not to wrinkle the double-breasted satin blazer Esme wore over a cream-colored blouse and black trousers.

Esme was always immaculately dressed, with her white hair perfectly styled in her signature bob. "Long time no see, Kat! I was in town and thought I'd stop by to see how Idlewyld is treating you."

Esme gestured to the chairs. Kat struggled with the idea of sitting when she should be working, but she couldn't refuse the renowned and respected Ms. Wilder.

"It's great. I love the job. It's so fulfilling."

"Is it?" Esme asked pensively. Her keen eyes fluttered across Kat's face in gentle yet knowing scrutiny. "How about other areas of your life? Do you see Nila much?"

"Oh, for sure!" Kat said. "I mean, she's busy with Pryce and with her new job, but we see each other..." She tried to recall when she last saw her best friend. Or talked with her on the phone... or even texted.

She couldn't remember.

"What about hobbies?" Esme continued to probe.

"My job is my hobby," Kat replied quickly.

"And... men?" Esme leaned forward as though they conspired over a great secret.

"Oh, well, you know. I'm a working lady. I don't have time for dating." Kat shrugged and laughed nervously. "I always say I'll look into a dating app when it slows down a bit here, but really? My life is fine. I take care of kids for a living. You can't really get better than that."

Esme's eyebrows knit together. "I remember a similar conversation with Nila. Nurses can love their jobs, but it's not all ups." Esme reached a hand out to rest it comfortingly on Kat's knee. "You do one of the hardest jobs there are."

"I try not to focus on the sad times, just look at the good. I mean, I accept them. Sure. But... it's not worth dwelling on. Not if I'm going to keep going."

"Sometimes, it's good to stop for a bit. Recharge. Rest."

Kat looked at Esme gravely and confessed something she hadn't dared to admit to even herself. "I'm afraid if I allow that, everything—all the stress, worries, fears—will come crashing down on top of me, and I won't be able to dig my way out of it."

"Kat..." Esme shook her head. "That will happen with or without your permission. Trust me. You can't outrun a dark cloud, but you *can choose* to stop and let it catch up with you, then deal with it on your own terms."

Kat looked away, ashamed of her admission.

"Your position comes with paid time off, doesn't it?" Esme asked. "Vacation and personal days?"

Kat nodded.

"Would I be right in assuming you haven't used a single one since you started?"

Kat nodded again.

"Well, that's perfect! I have an opportunity for you."

Kat opened her mouth to argue, but Esme kept going.

"Now, don't turn me down just yet, or I'll give you a whole speech about the research that's proven that time off decreases burnout and increases mental health. Do you need me to do that?"

"No, ma'am," Kat said. She was well aware of the statistics. She just didn't apply them to herself.

"Alright. To be fair, I'm asking for a favor, got it? It's perfectly suited for you. A pediatric nurse with nanny experience. Also..."

Esme got up and shut the door, then returned to her seat.

In a hushed tone, Esme finished, " A *shifter*."

Kat tilted her head to the side. It wasn't every day Esme Baer asked for a favor. It was especially unusual for it to be so secretive. "What's going on?"

Esme took a deep breath before explaining. "There is a child in need of some help right now. He witnessed a traumatic event, lost both of his parents, and shifted into his bobcat form. We're talking about a ten-year-old boy. And he hasn't shifted back."

"That's awful," Kat whispered, touching her hand to her mouth. "You want me to help him?"

Esme nodded. "He's with a guardian at the moment, but the man isn't experienced dealing with children, nor is he any kind of medical professional."

"Why was the boy placed with him, then?"

"Out of necessity," Esme replied gravely. "I suppose I need to clarify. His parents didn't die in some kind of accident. They were murdered... in front of him. The boy is being guarded right now because it's very likely the killer wants to get rid of the witness. The boy shifted into his bobcat and ran away to safety. Otherwise, the assailant would have undoubtedly..."

Esme trailed off, and Kat was grateful for it. She didn't want to hear the words.

"This is so horrible. That poor boy." Kat shook

her head, unable to imagine the pain the poor kid was feeling. "How long do you want me to work with him? Can this be an after-work thing?"

"Ideally, I'd like it if you could take a week or two off work," Esme said. "Not only would you be helping the boy and me out, but I have a feeling the HR department will be grateful they don't have to force you out of here to burn that time off."

"You're not wrong," Kat admitted. She received many emails, threatening her with forced vacation if she didn't use up her time off.. Esme's earlier words echoed through her mind. *On your own terms.* Better than being coerced into a week of listlessness. At least now, she could be useful. "Alright, I'll do it."

CHAPTER

TWO

High up in the Colorado mountains, the Cavalli organization's secluded cabins were hidden from view by a thick forest. A big brown bear paced the short and narrow dirt road that led to the wooden cottages. The beast harrumphed every time he turned back around and grumbled in annoyance. He didn't like waiting in *normal* circumstances.

Coleman Stride should've been happy in his natural habitat, surrounded by lush trees and a nearby pond.

He wasn't.

He wasn't here to enjoy the blissful quiet of nature. He was on a job. Not the kind of task that utilized his most honed abilities. Oh, no. For some reason—and despite being one of Oren Cavalli's best enforcers—he was now a glorified babysitter.

Literally.

He'd been tasked with the protection detail of important adults plenty of times before. In those cases, Coleman and his coworkers complained about the babysitting jobs.

But this time, he was *actually* watching over a child.

He eyed the little brown spotted bobcat warily. Though it was the size of a small house cat, it proved to be fast and wily when it ran from him. It was a pain in the ass for Coleman's large, ungainly bear form to chase. The thing could dart past the tree line and make it up any one of the Colorado pines before the lumbering bear could catch it.

Sure, Coleman's bear could roll a boulder up a hill without breaking a sweat, and he often prided himself on the strength. But when it came to dealing with a slippery cub, his brawniness was of no help.

And he hated anytime he was faced with a situation he or his bear couldn't excel at.

Hopefully, they'll send the nanny soon, he thought. Then the dang cub would be *her* problem, and Coleman could shift back into his human form to properly protect the property and the child.

His big bear body wasn't ideal for being a look-out. His human form could get around quicker, go to the house's second floor, and watch from that vantage point. The bear didn't have that kind of agility.

Unfortunately, the cub became terrified at the sight of Coleman's human version. It made sense since Coleman had an imposing stature meant to intimidate grown men. One look at Coleman and the bobcat darted off, quick and agile, far away from the cabin's safety.

Coleman had shifted into his bear for the heightened senses to sniff out the cub. That's when he learned that the little one wasn't as afraid when Coleman was a fellow animal. The bobcat—Jaylen Eppenger, Coleman reminded himself—came down from the tree. The cub reluctantly sat back on his haunches with a huff. His little eyes followed Coleman as he paced and paced, wearing down the path with every footfall. Eventually, Jaylen started to follow Coleman around like a little puppy.

When Coleman tried to shift back into human form, hoping the cub would see that he was the same bear and person, it made no difference. Jaylen tried running off, and Coleman had to turn back into a bear to chase him down. He grabbed him with his snout and carried him back to the cabin.

Finally, Jaylen tired himself out and curled close to Coleman, who continued his pacing. Watching. Waiting.

He was glad that they were sending backup because Coleman was about protection, not child-care. He could pick up the sound and scent of an enemy before they came close, chase them down through the densest trees or crowds, and shoot from almost a thousand yards away, but none of those skills helped a kid in need.

He nearly jumped for joy when the black car—one belonging to the Cavalli organization—pulled up to the cabin, but he didn't dare move. Jaylen was asleep, and he didn't want to wake the boy—especially since a stranger's presence might send him running again.

He watched from the back of the house as the driver—a house manager named Gia—walked the nanny into the cabin, noting that the woman was blonde and curvy, though he wasn't able to make out much more than that.

He waited while Gia likely showed the newcomer around inside. Gia knew more about the place than its owner—Oren—did, given that it was her job to care for the many different properties. She was the one responsible for stocking the place up with food and whatever else they needed while they looked after the kid.

Coleman nodded curtly when the two stepped out onto the back porch and spotted him. Gia turned to the nanny, said a few words, waved to Coleman, and left.

After a moment, the stranger cautiously made her way over to them.

Coleman, relieved at the arrival of his backup, slowly stood—slowly enough that he didn't wake Jaylen.

And he finally took a good look at the nanny, who was nearing him.

The blonde was absolutely beautiful—perfect in every way. She wasn't done up all fancy, like Oren's wife Anaya usually was. Instead, she looked like the shiny girl next door. Wholesome. Sweet. Caring.

Everything he shouldn't crave...

She sparkled under the setting sun's soft beams. Her blue eyes twinkled, the gloss on her full lips glimmered, and even her rosy dimpled cheeks glowed as she smiled at him. Her blonde hair shone as it tumbled off her shoulders when she waved tentatively. He longed to reach out and brush his fingers through the golden strands

Then her demeanor changed. Her eyes filled with pity when they landed on the bobcat. Her lips, the top one a perfect cupid's bow, tugged down into a frown, and Coleman swore he'd do anything to bring back her smile.

A strange feeling hit him and grew more intense the closer she stepped. It was as though he was dizzy and maybe about to fall, but also kind of drowning... Definitely like all the air had left his lungs, and he'd been kicked in the stomach.

She is ours.

It couldn't be true.

But it is. You know it's absolutely true.

Why was his fated mate walking toward him? Where had she come from, and why was she here now?

"Hi, I'm Kat," she whispered, crouching down, though, in his bear form, he was large enough to meet her eye-to-eye when she was standing.

Perhaps she's just used to dealing with alphas, and she knows she should crouch.

Out of necessity, because it was too overwhelming to be so near to her, he recoiled. He had to back away from her overwhelming scent of lilacs and freshwater. *So damned beautiful.*

"No, no, don't go!" she murmured, holding her hand out toward him.

The gesture, something so simple as reaching toward him, not even trying to grab him, but just moving to emphasize her words, should have been nothing. Just one stranger stretching a limb out toward another stranger.

Yet, Colman's entire being reacted as though it were *certainly something.* It was the strangest thing, but he froze in place, feeling *compelled* to reach out and grab her hand.

Because he saw *his mate* asking him to join her.

And this offered hand—specifically his mate's hand—*could not* be ignored.

He stepped toward her, ignoring the protests of his human rationality that reminded him that he was there on a job and, regardless, had no use for a mate.

His bear refused to play into that human cautionary nonsense. The very idea that one wouldn't embrace their *fated mate* on sight was incomprehensible to an animal. The animal didn't foresee the stress and worries that the human did. The beast didn't foresee the complications.

The animal just saw their perfect match and knew they were meant to be together.

Coleman made it just a few steps before Jaylen stirred, and suddenly both sides snapped together in agreement. *Fated mate can wait because our top priority, no matter what, is to protect the bobcat cub.*

The cub awoke and immediately snapped his head up toward Kat. His adverse reaction to her presence was fast. He hissed and growled and pulled his body into a tight spring. Coleman recognized Jaylen's reaction and responded instantly, grabbing the cub by his scruff. It was something he'd seen big cats do with their children on nature documentaries. The first time he'd tried it, he'd learned that not only did it prevent the cub from running away, but it also seemed to soothe the tiny beast.

Kat's blue eyes widened—becoming larger though he wouldn't have thought it possible. He starred at her, willing her to understand.

Humans scare him.

Somehow, she seemed to comprehend, and she began to strip. Coleman turned his head in a gesture of politeness. Though normally shifters didn't care about nudity, that fact didn't ring true for mates, and seeing her naked would certainly provoke thoughts that would prove distracting at a time like that.

While he looked away, he wondered, *Does she know I'm her mate too?*

He had almost no time to mull over it. Something bumped him, and he turned.

Another cat. This one wooly and grey.

He usually disliked anything that wasn't a bear.

But this one is my mate. Look at her!

For the first time in his life, he admired the strength and beauty of a lynx, from her enormous paws all the way up to the long tufts on the top of her ears. He even noted that her fluffy nub tail was cute—it sort of reminded him of the stump he had on his own bear backside.

While he was lost in thought, she came back around and nudged his muzzle, and he realized she was urging him to drop Jaylen. The cub couldn't flee and had stopped its growls and hisses of protest to settle as a passive puppet in Coleman's maw.

The cub probably quieted as soon as she'd shifted, though Coleman was too distracted to notice.

Satisfied that Jaylen was calm, he set him on the ground and released him. Coleman sat back on his haunches, expecting the cub to run into his side and cuddle up like he usually did.

Instead, the traitor abandoned Coleman and went straight to Kat. The little brownish-orange spotted bobcat circled the bigger grey cat, sniffing her and even batting at her to test out his new friend.

Coleman didn't know much about cats, but he could note the differences between the two different species. The bobcat had sleeker fur with spots and paws proportionate to his body. It also had a short tail—not a quarter of the length you'd think a cat's tail should be—but it was at least slightly more substantial than the one on the lynx.

Coleman rumbled to his feet, making a playful protesting noise. *You just leaving me already, kid?*

In response, the bobcat bounded back over to him, circling him, and then laid down between Coleman and Kat.

The cub was sleepy, exhausted by all the excitement. The two adults eyed each other. Coleman rolled his big shaggy bear shoulders in a kind of shrug and then lay down.

Kat followed, and the two of them faced each other with the bobcat adjacent to their snouts.

CHAPTER

THREE

Kat lay almost snout-to-snout with her fated mate.

My fated mate!

Esme was a world-renowned matchmaker specializing in shifter mates. Kat knew this was a set-up. Esme purposely didn't tell Kat her mate would be here, knowing Kat would turn down the job. Kat would have refused to meet her mate, would have protested that she had too much going on in her life, and couldn't possibly deal with such a complication.

Would I have, though? Glancing at Jaylen, her heart tugged intensely, and she couldn't bear the thought of denying aid to the kitten. That little one needed help, and lynx to bobcat, Kat was the best option.

Though the bear—her fated mate—sure looked absolutely adorable curled up with the kitten. And the way he'd grabbed Jaylen before he ran off? Instincts a mother lynx could definitely approve of. Especially impressive since bears weren't usually that quick or agile.

Noticing that Jaylen was finally sleeping, Kat locked eyes with Coleman. The bear moved his big head in a sort of nod and rose to his feet slowly. Kat followed. A few feet away from the kitten, the pair shifted back into their human form before silently gathering their clothes. Finally dressed, they stood close together while keeping a wary eye on the sleeping bobcat.

They didn't bother with introductions or pleasantries. They were perfectly in sync when it came to caring for the boy.

"What happens if we pick him up? Will he wake as soon as we move him?" Kat asked.

"I haven't tried doing that, but he hates the sight of humans. I have no idea how he'd react." Coleman said. As he spoke, Kat struggled against the distraction of his alluring scent. Her *mate's* scent. It reminded her of pine and sandalwood—a sensual combination of a forest and a beach.

"So if we're human out here in the woods, we

risk him running and getting too far away. What about if we bring him inside?"

"He'd tear up a room."

She nodded. "Perfect. At least he won't be able to get away. Go inside, clear out a room of all breakables. I'll bring him in."

"What if he wakes and starts flailing? He's going to be strong—"

"Uh, pediatric nurse and also a lynx here. I can handle a bobcat kitten."

"Cub."

"What?" Her eyes narrowed in confusion.

"He's a bobcat cub." He shrugged.

"No. Bobcat kitten. Bears are cubs. Ugh, never mind, it's not important. We don't have time for this. Go clear out a room, and I'll bring him in." She laughed a little and shook her head, though it dawned on her that the bear calling Jaylen a cub was a sign, in some strange way, that Coleman had kind of claimed him as his own.

Or maybe he's just not been around anything but bears.

Either way, she found it goofy and endearing, but they needed to move Jaylen in before it was completely dark outside.

Kat wasn't a mother, but she'd dealt with so many children in her job that she had something of a mother's touch. Using those skills, she maneuvered the kitten into her arms. She was right to be confident because her plan worked. The little one didn't stir while she picked him up, brought him inside, and walked toward the room Coleman pointed her toward.

"This one was the most empty already," Coleman whispered.

"Perfect. Now barricade the door and then get on the bed," Kat murmured as she walked past him and into the room.

"What?"

"Push that dresser over the door to ensure he can't jiggle the handle in a panic. Then, get on the bed." She placed Jaylen in the middle of the bed and laid to one side. She gestured to the other, arching a warning brow at him to comply.

She was in full boss mode.

Coleman hesitated. She thought perhaps he would try to make some kind of alpha stand and insist that he wouldn't take orders from her. But, he relented and followed her instructions. He effortlessly picked up the dresser, impressing her with his strength. At least he hadn't pushed it over, making a whole lot of noise and risking waking Jaylen before they were ready.

Then, with physical grace that should be impossible in a man his size, Coleman carefully crept onto the bed next to her.

The sight was nearly too much. Already she found him incredibly attractive, but in the low light of the bedroom, lying so close to him, she could make out all of his enticing features. Black hair, short on the sides and a bit longer on top. Dark, thick eyebrows and a short but dense mustache and beard. Eyes sharp and piercing. A sharp jawline. Thick and muscular arms that would be perfect for holding her...

"If we sleep like this, he'll get used to our scent," she whispered, explaining her theory while trying to stop admiring Coleman's form. "When he wakes, he might not be so startled and upset by our presence."

"And if you're wrong and he wakes up and throws a fit?"

"I'm not wrong," Kat said confidently. "But if he does, so what? He trashes the room until he tires himself out. Even shifter kittens have to recharge."

"Alright."

She lay across from Coleman, her head on the pillow and Jaylen between them at chest level. With

Coleman's head on the other pillow, they had a clear sight of one another. It was a surprisingly intimate situation for someone she'd just met, yet Kat yearned to reach her hand out and feel her fingers intertwine with his. They didn't know each other. She only knew his name because the driver, Gia, filled her in on all the details.

Gia hadn't informed Kat that Coleman would be her mate, but the woman wouldn't have known that.

Only Esme knew that little piece of the puzzle.

Damn you, Esme.

Kat finally had her life figured out. She had her routine. One consisting of an eighty-hour work-week, sure, but it was satisfying. Now, what was she supposed to do?

Esme had just really wanted to show her what she was missing by being a workaholic...

Thank you, Esme.

KAT AWOKE to a gentle nudge on her shoulder.

Bleary-eyed, she assessed her surroundings and saw that her prediction was only off a little, but her instincts had been right on.

She'd assumed that if the kitten slept surrounded by their human scents, he would become familiar with them and then perhaps not panic when he woke.

She hadn't dared to hope that it would work so well that he would turn back into his human form. But sure enough, Coleman lay in his spot across from her, shirtless, and between them lay a sleeping little boy, clad in the bodyguard's oversized black t-shirt. The boy's light brown hair was shaggy and tousled, and his little sleeping face was angelic. Kat's heart swelled at the sight of him.

Sensing eyes on her, she looked up at Coleman. Their gazes hooked, leaving them both quiet and frozen in a perfect bubble of peace and familiarity.

"If we wake him, we will startle him," Kat whispered softly. "But I think if we start to talk to each other, gently at first and then increasing to normal levels, it might do the same thing our scents did. Allow him to become familiar with the sound of us, so he comes to without being jarred."

"You're pretty smart," Coleman said in a matching volume, though his carried a growly, rumbling note that sent chills down her spine. "How do you know to do all this stuff?"

"I'm a pediatric nurse," Kat replied, getting a

little louder. "But I've studied a lot of child psychology. It helps a lot when you work with kids as much as I do. Especially in hospital settings. They're not in a great situation, so we figure out the best ways to help them feel more at ease."

"I shouldn't be surprised that Oren found the absolute best person to send up here. Not only do you have the nurse and psychology thing going, but you're a cat shifter too. I had no idea Oren's networks were that good."

"He had help outside his normal networks." Kat shook her head and rolled her eyes. "Ever heard of Esme Baer?"

"Name sounds familiar."

"She's the one that came to the hospital and suggested I take this job. Apparently, she's the one who found Jaylen and brought him to Oren and put your name up for guard duty."

"She did? How did she know that I should…"

"She's a matchmaker."

"What?"

"Finds shifters their fated mates, specifically."

"No shit?" He covered his mouth at the curse word, blushing. Kat's heart fluttered, her breath caught up in a wave of attraction. "I thought they sent me on this duty because I have the same history as him..." He trailed off, avoiding her eyes while his impromptu confession hung between them.

Kat surmised what history they could share. Coleman was a bear, Jaylen was a bobcat, so it wasn't their animals.

Her heart dropped as it dawned on her. Was Coleman also an orphan? Had he seen his parents murdered?

Her eyes widened, but Coleman put his finger to his lips and then pointed down to Jaylen, who'd started to stir. The child glanced up, his soulful little brown eyes going first to Kat, then to Coleman, then back up to the ceiling.

With a big yawn, he sat up in bed. Coleman and Kat followed.

"Where am I?" Jaylen asked, looking around the room. "Why do I feel like I know you? I don't, or do I? Do I have amnesia or something?"

"My name is Kat, and this is Coleman," Kat said. "Do you know your name?"

"Jaylen."

"So, not quite amnesia. Can you tell me what month and year it is?"

Kat ran through a series of questions that were used for amnesia patients. Based on his answers,

Jaylen's last memory was the night before his parents were killed.

"My parents are dead, though," he said after a moment. "I... I don't know how I know that, but..." His little chin quivered as his eyes lined with tears. His small hand reached for Kat's, and he gripped it tightly. "It's true, isn't it? They're dead, and I'm here with you because you're taking care of me now."

Kat pressed her lips together and nodded. "Yes."

"You okay?" Coleman asked.

"I.... yeah... I think so," Jaylen replied, his face scrunching up in thought. "Like, I know this is weird, right? I know this thing, this really bad, sad thing, but it feels like... Like when you lose a video game, and you're really upset at first, but then later it's okay... Like I was upset, but I don't remember being upset, and now it's okay."

"That's fine, Jaylen," Kat encouraged. "You don't have to think about it too much, but we're here for you if you do want to, okay?"

"Okay." He nodded and scooted off the bed. "I have to go to the bathroom."

Coleman moved the dresser and showed him the way.

While they waited outside the door, Kat and Coleman discussed the situation in hushed tones.

"Sounds like his bobcat side processed the trauma for him," Kat said. "We have no way of knowing if the memories are permanently missing or if it's just a temporary block. He could eventually remember and experience the pain and grief in his human form. But for now, maybe this is what he needs to do to survive."

"Yeah. Survive." Coleman grunted, crossing his legs and looking out the window.

Was he thinking about his own tragic childhood? Kat didn't pry. If Coleman wanted to share, he could. In the meantime, she'd be satisfied knowing that Esme had definitely found the right people to help the boy.

FOUR

COLEMAN COULDN'T HAVE BEEN MORE RELIEVED THAT Kat's plan worked. Jaylen was back in boy form for now. It made their job easier in many ways, but surprisingly, Coleman was mostly glad because he wanted the boy to be okay. And being in human form seemed like a first step toward that.

They showed Jaylen the upstairs room upstairs that was prepared for him. The previous day, Anaya Cavalli sent up car after car filled with clothes, toys, and books. There was even a video game console connected to the Wi-Fi and preloaded with Oren's credit card. They could buy whatever games Jaylen wanted.

That was a mama bear in action.

Jaylen picked out some clothes and then went to

the adjoining bathroom to shower. Coleman took the quiet opportunity to patrol the property while Kat prepared breakfast.

As Coleman walked around the house's perimeter, he ensured there were no strange scents or footprints. He caught sight of the beautiful blonde through the kitchen window on his way back.

She really is something, our mate.

In the light of a new day, with the biggest concern resolved—Jaylen no longer stuck as a bobcat—Coleman could finally really think about Kat.

He could get all turned around about his fated mate and what that meant to him.

He'd never wanted a mate before. He had plenty of women at his disposal, and that meant that he could live a no-strings-attached life. A mate? That was a complication he never wanted. He grew up a loner. How could anyone expect him to change? No one ever asked when he would be home. No one cared if Oren sent him off on a trip to god-knows-where without any notice. And he never wished for someone who would worry for him. Someone who cared if he was around.

Lies.

Deep inside of him, something tugged at his

heart. An uncomfortable feeling that he was used to pushing down and ignoring.

Loneliness.

He growled to himself and decided maybe it was best to not think about Kat. Re-entering the house, it took great effort for him to only barely glance at her when he strode through the kitchen and announced, "Everything looks fine out there."

He went upstairs and took a seat in the open loft area, waiting for Jaylen to emerge.

"I'm hungry. Do I smell food?" Jaylen asked when he walked out of his room wearing jeans and a tan hoodie.

The colors reminded him of a bobcat, but Coleman couldn't have been happier seeing the little boy look like a normal kid.

"Yeah, Kat's been making a feast down there," he replied, motioning for Jaylen to lead them downstairs.

"I feel like I could eat a lot."

"Me too. As a bear, I can always eat a lot."

Jaylen nodded. "Yeah. I kind of know you're a bear. A big brown one, right? I don't remember how I know that, but I know that. Kat, she's a big grey cat, right?"

"A lynx," she answered for herself, meeting them

at the bottom of the stairs and directing them to the large dining room table. "Now, eat up. Don't worry about being stuffed because after, we're going to go lay on the couch and just watch TV like good lazy cats."

"I'm a cat?" he asked, looking up at them quizzically.

"You remember I'm a bear, and she's a lynx, but not that you're a bobcat?"

"Now that you mention it..." The little boy scrunched up his face in deep thought. "I do know that I'm a bobcat. Like my parents. But how do *you* know? Was I in my cat form? I kind of think I remember that I was. Was that a dream?"

Kat and Coleman exchanged glances. "No, it wasn't a dream," Kat said. "But you don't have to think too much about it now, okay? Just eat."

Jaylen didn't need any more encouragement to dig into the chocolate chip pancakes, scrambled eggs, and bacon. Kat grabbed two coffee mugs and handed one to Coleman, using her chin to gesture toward the sliding kitchen doors that led to the back porch. They needed a moment to talk privately, away from little ears that already went through too much.

Coleman took a sip. "Black coffee with sugar. How'd you know?"

"You're a bear. That means strong, but also with a sweet tooth." She shrugged and smiled. Her perfect pink lips pulled up to reveal her dimples, lighting up her face.

It stirred a warmth inside him. Given the chance, he wanted to bask in her glow forever. Ignoring his feelings for her was no easy feat. Not when she smiled like that and revealed a talent for guessing his favorite coffee order.

"I'm starting to think you're psychic."

"Just perceptive about the world around me, with a mind that remembers things about people and makes associations from one to the other."

"Right..."

"Now what?" Kat wondered aloud. "I was hired for two weeks to stay up here and care for Jaylen, but they also said it might not be that long, depending on how things go. What does that mean?"

"We're up here till the person responsible is dealt with," Coleman grunted.

Kat's pink lips formed an O, and her eyes widened.

He could have been more vague, made it sound

like maybe they were waiting for the cops to arrest the guy, but he had no reason to dilute the truth. If she was going to work for Oren, if she was going to be around Coleman for any length of time, then she needed to know exactly what kind of people they were.

"You're here to care for the boy," Coleman continued. "I'm here for protection. This situation is serious. The man who took out Jaylen's parents *will* come after him. He has to. Otherwise, his job is unfinished, and he's a failure."

"Come after a *kid,* though? Who would do that?"

"People we protect others against. That's what Oren hires me and the others for. To protect people, no matter the cost," he added bitterly. "There's a lot of evil in this world."

He hated the horror that filled her eyes, but it was necessary. Especially considering she was his mate. There would be danger. His mate needed to be warned, so she didn't do something dumb and get herself killed.

Mate.

"We should talk about it, shouldn't we?" she asked, almost reading his mind. Or perhaps she was looking for a change of subject. "The mate thing."

He took another sip of his coffee and didn't answer. He didn't know what to say.

"You feel it too, don't you? The fated mates pull?" she asked, looking up at him with such wide blue innocent eyes that he had to look away.

"What of it?" he snapped. "You're attractive. I'm attracted. But it's a moot point. We have a job to do, and we're going to focus on that. We'll ignore these primal instincts and do what we're here for."

He felt her deflate, her hope wilting because of his words. His body could sense what hers was feeling—such was the way with fated mates.

"Oh," Kat said, her tone soft. "That's how you feel about it? That it was just attraction? Not like, oh, I don't know, like your whole world shattered? Like everything's changed, and you're left with an absolute certainty that this was the shifter made for you?"

He finally turned back toward her, seeing that her eyes had dropped, and his heart tugged at him. He didn't want to upset her. He didn't want to lie to her.

He also didn't want to consider the possibilities because he'd always accepted the fact that he'd lived alone. It was too risky to think about a life with Kat. Risky for her because of his job, risky for him because he'd spent twenty years hardening his heart.

"Kat, please don't feel like you're rejected. I'm just focused on my job. Two people were murdered, you know? And the kid is a target." He sighed and steadied himself after the shock of admitting this to her. He wasn't reconciled with it, but she needed this. His *mate* needed this. It was all he could offer her, so he spoke softly. "You *do* make me feel something intense. Otherworldly. Destined... I could absolutely lose all of myself in these feelings I'm having for you. That's exactly why I have to ignore them, at least for right now. I can't drop my guard and let someone get the kid, you know?"

As he explained his reasoning, he realized how true it was. Somewhere his subconscious pushed forward, insisting that he do the job first and not lose himself in his beautiful and alluring mate.

A faint smile returned to her lips. "I can appreciate that... like, a lot. I want to do all I can for him, too."

"Then we focus on him." He nodded, and it sealed their understanding.

As promised, the two cats took over the couches after breakfast, lounging while Jaylen took control of the remote. Coleman excused himself and checked in with Oren, then walked around the property, glad he could be back at his normal job.

It wasn't a half-hour before he was overcome with boredom.

He returned to the living room area, hearing Kat and Jaylen talk.

"What do you like to do for fun?" Kat's sweet tone asked.

"Video games."

Coleman peered into the room, seeing both of them relaxed, each on their own couch, sunbeams streaming in through the windows to bathe them.

"There is a game system here. Do they have any games you like?"

Jaylen shrugged.

"They set it up so you can download some."

Jaylen's face lit up, and he ran to the cabinet to check it out.

Seeing they didn't need him, Coleman continued to wander around.

Walking.

Sitting.

Walking.

Sitting.

Watching through the windows as Kat and Jaylen played video games.

They can't do that for two weeks straight...

His gaze turned to the big storage shed, and an idea hit him.

He spent the next few hours setting up his plan—including calling out for some deliveries—and then went in for lunch when Kat called. She'd made hefty sandwiches with lots of meat and veggies on thick bread.

"Eat up, kid," Coleman instructed. "You're going to need the fuel for what I have ready for you outside."

"Outside?" Jaylen asked, scrunching up his nose in distaste. "But we have video games inside."

"A young boy can't spend all his time inside with a controller. You need to get outside and get some real experience."

"Coleman..." Kat started.

"Trust me, I know what a boy needs."

She conceded with a barely noticeable nod.

After lunch, they worked as a team to clean the kitchen. Before Jaylen could scamper off to play video games, Coleman ushered him outside. Kat trailed behind, curious and cautious.

"This, Jaylen, is your training center."

Coleman showed him what all he'd set up. "I have all these haybales here with targets on them, and you have three different kinds of projectile weapons: axes, bows, and guns."

"Guns!" Kat shrieked. "No, Coleman, I—"

"*Nerf* guns," Coleman clarified. "Though, much as I think he's old enough to use a real one, I figured starting with foam bullets would be best."

Kat pursed her lips and crossed her arms. He could see the fury emanating off of her, but she said nothing else as Coleman set Jaylen up at the first station. When the kid started to get the hang of it, Coleman walked over to Kat.

"Was this Oren's idea?" she asked.

"No, Oren didn't tell me to do this. I did it because I was there myself. I know what the kid needs. This wasn't me just thinking up fun stuff for him to do. I'm trying to help him."

"Helping him is letting him feel like a normal kid," Kat argued.

"This is normal kid activities to do out at the cottage," Coleman objected. "Outdoorsy shit. That's the point of leaving town and going up into the mountains."

She looked at Jaylen, who actually enjoyed hurling the ax at the target. "On one hand, it's kinda sweet that you've thought to do this for him," Kat replied.

"And on the other hand?"

"On the other hand, the kid is *ten*. And he was perfectly happy sitting inside and playing video games."

Coleman took a few steps further back and lowered his voice when Kat followed. "Video games aren't going to help him if he's in danger."

"Why would he be in danger? Are people going to be gunning for him once you take his parent's killer off the street?"

"No," Coleman admitted. "Oren's intel is that he was acting alone and chose his victims randomly to try to prove himself. Once he's gone, no one will pick up his mission. But that's beside the point. This whole situation has changed Jaylen's life forever, and he's got to be ready for them."

"He's just a kid," Kat protested.

"No, he's not *just a kid*. Because not every kid is born in Idlewyld, and not every kid in Idlewyld has their parents murdered in front of their eyes."

Kat blinked in shock, obviously hating the idea. "Oren will find him a home, somewhere safe. Somewhere outside Idlewyld."

"Maybe," Coleman shrugged. "Or maybe he'll get a family in Idlewyld. Or maybe he'll end up like I did. Passed around from one temporary home to another. Either way, these kinds of activities help build confidence as well as strength, which he's going to need to *survive*."

"I'd argue with you," Kat said, her jaw set tight. "But... I'm giving you the benefit of the doubt. I can quote from child psychology textbooks and research articles, but you seem to be making suggestions based on personal experience. Who's to say who's right? So, how about this? We compromise. Split the days, fifty-fifty? He can do some of your activities half the time, and the other half I get to indulge and spoil him with video games and cupcakes."

"Cupcakes?"

"I make a mean cupcake," she broke her stare from Jaylen to smile up at Coleman, and his whole being melted. He itched to take her face in his hands and pull her into a kiss.

Focus on the kid right now. The woman later, They'd agreed on that already. He had to keep his word because there was no way he was going to let himself kiss her. He would get lost in her lips and then have their enemy take that moment to ambush them.

CHAPTER
FIVE

True to his word, Coleman allowed them to split their free time. They fell into a routine. After eating breakfast together, Jaylen spent the morning playing video games or binging television. After lunch, the kid went outside to exert his energy and, as Coleman put it, learn some survival skills and increase his confidence. Jaylen was usually quiet at dinner, exhausted from his physical activities. The three of them lounged in front of the TV before bedtime. It was all very domestic, but Jaylen was doing better. That was the most important thing.

Kat thought that Coleman would stick to the little training area he'd set up, but he surprised them by taking them down to the pond.

"Today, you're going to learn how to row and

steer a boat, water safety, and fishing," Coleman told Jaylen while he handed them fishing poles.

Kat's looked like it was used. It was probably kept at the cabin, but the child-sized one he handed Jaylen was definitely new.

Fishing?!

Nope.

"What's wrong?" Coleman asked when they approached the pond where the little rowboat waited.

"Lynxes are great at catching fish, but we usually do it from the safety of dry land," Kat answered.

She could have stayed behind and let the boys go fishing on their own, but her protective instinct didn't want to let Jaylen go out there by himself. Well, of course, Coleman would be with him, and she trusted Coleman... Didn't she?

He wouldn't chuck the boy overboard to teach him some swimming survival, would he?

She didn't think so, but she also didn't really know Coleman all *that* well. She reluctantly loaded into the boat with the guys and settled uneasily. She gripped the side for dear life the entire time they were out there.

Coleman was a kind mentor, patiently teaching Jaylen how to use the oars and hold the fishing rod.

She no longer worried that he would pull the "sink or swim" tactic, but nothing eased her discomfort of being on the water.

"Too bad there isn't a dock," Jaylen spoke up. "Then we wouldn't have to be in the boat, and Kat could enjoy fishing more."

"You're enjoying fishing?" Kat asked.

Jaylen smiled sheepishly. "I am, but I think I'd like it if there was a dock too. Could you build us a dock, Coleman?" Jaylen pleaded.

Kat snorted a laugh. "Oh, sorry. Just the thought of Coleman building things..."

"He told me it's one of his favorite hobbies," Jaylen said.

Kat's head turned toward Coleman in surprise. "Really?"

He shrugged. "Everyone needs a hobby."

Kat nodded. "Right." Esme had said something like that too, but Kat didn't have a hobby.

"So, can you do it?" The little boy blinked hopefully, every bat of his lashes cuter than the last.

Coleman looked back to shore and scratched his head. "Well, a floating dock would be easy, but I'm guessing that would be more bouncing than you felines are comfortable with. If Oren can get someone to come by and install the posts and drop off the supplies, then yeah, we could do it."

"Yes, let's do it!" Jaylen clapped his hands excitedly.

It was the first time he was excited about something. Kat and Coleman couldn't turn him down.

"I'll call Oren and get it all set up."

Despite her discomfort in the boat, Kat was glad she was there to see how thrilled Jaylen became when he hooked a fish. They had plenty of fish to feed a bear and two cats for dinner by the time they were done. There would even be some leftovers. Coleman explained that the cabin was a Cavalli bear clan spot—Oren loaned it out to different bear families who wanted some time out of the city—and they kept the pond well-stocked, considering bears really loved their fish.

When they rowed back to shore, Kat expected Jaylen to run off to play video games, but this time he didn't.

"Can I help you clean them?" he asked Coleman once he'd helped tie up the boat.

"I'm out on that one." Kat shuddered. She'd never liked to watch the fish be prepared.

"How do you know you won't like it till you try

it?" Jaylen asked, parroting a line Coleman had told him at least once in the past two days.

"I *have* tried it," Kat explained. "The clowder I grew up in lived around a lake, and fishing was a normal pastime. I fished when I was a kid, but I never liked the ickiness of the preparation process. Chalk it up to cats liking to be clean." She shrugged and excused herself, taking advantage of the moment to go inside and have a shower.

When she emerged, Jaylen was just trudging in, looking a little green.

"Icky?" Kat asked.

He shrugged sheepishly. "Kinda."

"Go have a shower. We'll have dinner soon."

Kat continued on to the kitchen, where she found Coleman hard at work. It was quite sexy to see the usually gruff and stoic bodyguard, clad in an apron, the figure of domesticity while he prepared the food for Kat and Jaylen. He expertly arranged the trout on tinfoil, entirely at ease adding lemon slices and fresh herbs to the packs.

"So, woodworking isn't your only hobby," Kat teased, taking a seat at one of the island barstools. "Looks like cooking might be one of them too."

The man smiled—a rare sight that warmed her

right up. "Learning to cook meant tasty meals... who wouldn't like that?"

"You kept the fish whole."

"I did some fillets for later. They're in the fridge, but I thought tonight we can do fire safety and cook them outside in the pit."

Kat didn't point out that he was encroaching on the video game time once again. She could definitely see how he'd been right about it being good for Jaylen to do so much outdoors. The kid was having a good time.

They talked and flirted, and she almost felt like something bloomed between them. Before it could really develop roots, a freshly showered Jaylen joined them. Coleman moved toward the door as though Kat didn't exist anymore. "Alright, kid, let's hit it. Then you can be proud that you fed yourself, start to finish. Catching, prepping, and cooking. It will be the best meal you've ever had."

Kat stayed behind, watching out the window as Coleman and Jaylen started a fire and then placed the fish packets in the pit around it.

Kat finished cooking the rice and veggies that Coleman had started and brought them outside. The three ate a meal together—a very delicious one—

and then Kat revealed that she found marshmallows, graham crackers, and chocolate in the pantry.

"I guess if you can do video games at home anytime, that's why you wouldn't want to do them up here, huh?" Jaylen mused while they listened to the crackling fire and gazed up at the stars. "There are so many different things to do here."

CHAPTER

SIX

Coleman was glad he chose the room right next to Jaylen's because that night, he woke to terrible sounds coming from the boy's room.

Coleman burst into Jaylen's room just as Kat ran up the stairs. They found Jaylen in his bobcat form, running in every direction, tearing up anything that got in his way.

"He must be having a nightmare," Kat surmised.

"He's out of control," Coleman replied, reaching to take his shirt off.

Kat placed a hand on his arm, "No, let me."

Kat quickly pulled off her pajamas and shifted into her lynx form. It took her seconds to wrestle Jaylen and grab him by the scruff of his neck.

At first, Jaylen fought and flailed, but the neck hold did the trick, calming him down.

Coleman was wary that his human form would incite another round of terror, but to his surprise, when Kat set the cub—kitten—down in front of him, he only looked up at Coleman.

He swore he saw helplessness in the cat's eyes.

"Jaylen, can you shift back?"

The bobcat didn't move.

"You can't control it yet? But do you understand what I'm saying? Nod your head if you can."

He did.

Coleman exchanged a look with the lynx. This was more than he'd been able to do when he was last stuck in bobcat form.

Not only was he not scared of humans, but he seemed to be somewhat conscious.

Not knowing what else to do, Coleman sat on the ground next to Jaylen, with Kat taking the other side. He started to pet the bobcat, speaking softly to him, hoping his voice was calming and soothing.

"We all have nightmares," Coleman said. "I know I do. But they're just dreams. The way I look at them, they're our brains' way of practicing. Not that we'd ever be chased by a T-Rex or whatever was going on with you..."

The lynx snapped a look at him as if to say, *let's not put new potential nightmare ideas into his head, okay?*

"Okay, okay," Coleman nodded and continued talking to Jaylen. "It's all pretend, and it's just your brain's way of doing some preparation for something that's never going to happen because you're safe now. Kat and I will always keep you safe."

The moment he said it, he realized he misspoke using the word *always*. He didn't correct it to *for the next week or two*, though. Jaylen didn't need to hear that just then. Not when he was finally settling down, curled on the carpet, his heart rate slowing down to normal.

"Now, let's think about how you feel right now, okay? You see those paws? And those spots?" Coleman asked, pointing at the spots on the bobcat's paw. "Those belong to your bobcat form. But see my fingers?"

He placed his hand next to the little bobcat paw to demonstrate. "You want to think about having fingers. Kat, how about you shift back?"

The lynx stood, going to the doorway where she left her clothes. She shifted with her back to them, and Coleman turned his head, not wanting to let her naked body distract him from helping Jaylen.

"I just had to think about how I wanted to be a human again." Kat sat down next to them, clad in her pajamas.

It worked. Jaylen turned back from a bobcat into a boy. Colman was stunned. He helped the boy back into his pajamas while Kat asked him how he felt.

"Weird, I guess. I was a bobcat. I remember it this time."

"Do you remember your dream? What scared you?" Kat asked.

"No."

"Do you remember anything from the last time you'd shifted?" Kat followed up.

"No."

Kat nodded, though Coleman could see the sympathy in her eyes for Jaylen. "Alright, well, do you want to go to sleep, or..."

"Yes, I want to sleep. I'm tired." No sooner did he crawl into bed than he was completely out. Coleman and Kat waited around for a bit to make sure he was okay, then quietly snuck out.

"He remembers being a cat," Coleman stated as they walked down the stairs.

"It means he was more present this time than he was before."

"The cat and human are complete strangers

right now. They need to spend time together to become one."

Kat agreed. "Usually, when kids start to step into their shift, the animal has been around for a while, uniting with the human soul. For Jaylen, he was pushed into it unprepared. We shouldn't worry. They'll start becoming one body and mind."

The adrenaline was still pumping in Coleman's veins from the scare of it, and he knew it was for Kat too.

"We put his ability to shift out of mind. At least I did. Hadn't given it a second thought. I guess I thought it was a one-off deal. Just a heat of the moment thing," Coleman admitted.

"Yeah, me too, I guess," Kat mused. "But it doesn't seem that way. It's been activated and will be there for him whenever panic sets in."

"Will make it hard for him to go to a school with non-shifters. If he can't control it." Coleman's worry was palpable.

Kat nodded. "There are all-shifter schools. There's always homeschooling."

"Less opportunity for any semblance of normalcy," Coleman muttered.

"Well, we'll need to help him. I've heard of some meditative exercises for people unable to connect to their shift on their own. That's all adult stuff, though. For those who've shifted on their own but had some trauma that made them unable to connect."

"That's not going to help a kid who's never shifted on his own before."

"Right."

"We need to teach him to control his shift by testing his bravery. Challenge his bravery to trigger the instinct. Like what brought on the shifts before."

"Uh, no. First of all, putting a kid in risky situations is a bad idea. And second, if he's looking for it —for the feeling of his animal inside—preparing for the feeling to shift, it will never come."

"Well, then I'll prep some shock—"

"No, you won't," Kat gasped. "We're not going to try scaring the heck out of the kid."

They sat in silence again, contemplating.

Finally, Kat asked, "Did the same thing happen to you? With your shifting ability?"

Coleman stiffened at her question. He'd alluded to the fact that he'd been an orphan like Jaylen, but this was the first time Kat directly prodded him.

When he didn't answer, she scooted over, gently brushing her fingers over his arm, which was stretched out over the back of the couch.

"I know we've put the boy first, and I gotta tell you, that's something I really like. But now, maybe it's time that we break the seal between Working together will take everything we have. We need to do it for Jaylen. To find what will help him. I have the expertise, you have the experience, but we're not using all of our resources if you don't share what you know."

He didn't recoil from her words or her touch. In fact, he let the gentle grazing of her fingers relax him in a way he'd never felt before. The intimacy of it, the caring behind it...

It was his mate touching him. Kat's proximity, her skin against his sent jolts of relaxation in all of his nerve endings. He had once believed that fated mates were about a purely sexual connection, but now he knew it wasn't. Not when she caressed him so sweetly.

He sighed. "I can share my experience, but to be fair, I was older than Jaylen. My mother was already out of the picture. She abandoned us when I was born. My father did his best to raise me, but he was really only a kid himself. We couch surfed a lot. He was in different biker gangs. And then, one day, we were in front of our house, and..."

He shrugged, seeing the memory so clearly in his mind's eye. His body instinctively tightened.

He hadn't been lucky like Jaylen. He'd remembered every second of it. Always.

"I did shift when it happened, but it was a drive-by. They didn't stay around to take me out too, so I didn't have to flee. I guess because I was older than Jaylen by a bit—I was thirteen, so probably likely going to start shifting in the next few years anyway—I maintained consciousness. My animal didn't need to take over to protect me."

"I'm so sorry," Kat whispered.

He shrugged. "I've had a lot of time to process it. Therapy, believe it or not. That's Oren's doing."

"Really? I mean, Oren sounds like a great guy, taking care of folks and all. I didn't take him for the therapy type."

"Oh yeah. He's all about mental health as an issue. How we all need to be in control of our mental faculties or else we don't control anything."

"So you went with Oren after your father died?"

"No, I didn't know him back then. I floated from one couch to another until I was seventeen. That's when I met Oren, and he took me in."

"Oh."

"Before I met him, I stayed with other shifters.

Since I'd shifted once, they assumed I could just do it. But no one actually taught me. They just took me along to clan events, and when everyone shifted, I either did or didn't. I was embarrassed not to do it, though, so…" He tried to remember. Shifting was second nature to him now, so it was hard to remember back to when it wasn't. "I guess I remember closing my eyes and asking my bear to please come out so I wouldn't be embarrassed in front of the others. Now, the bear and I are one and the same, but back then, I had to talk to it, call it out."

Kat nodded. "Good. You can tell Jaylen that. See if it helps him."

"Which means we need to help the boy practice shifting."

"Yeah," she agreed. "He's so young, and I hate the idea of forcing his shift. But the alternative is that he shifts unexpectedly without being able to change back, then it's what we need to do."

After a moment of quiet, her hand stilled on his arm. He looked at her. "And you, Kat? You had a normal childhood?"

"What is normal?" She laughed a little and averted her gaze. "I had a big family, full of sisters, and we grew up in a community of lynxes. I thought that was normal, but since leaving, going to school, and becoming a nurse, I don't think I've met anyone else who grew up similarly."

"A community of lynxes?"

"A community of anything. That seems so rare nowadays, you know? But back then, we'd all get together for big barbecues, birthday parties, weddings, whatever. It was like a big extended family. It was a utopia, really, looking back on it now."

"Why'd you leave?"

"I just thought that's what you do," she mused. "Pick a profession and go out into the world. Find your mate. Make a new family for yourself outside the clowder."

"Do you ever think about going back?"

She blinked at that one and then shook her head. "No, I never really considered it. I've been so laser-focused on my career. That's all I think about. I moved to Idlewyld because my friend Nila did. I was also offered a job that was an advancement for my career, so I took it."

"And are you happy?"

"I thought I was... Are you? Happy?"

Somehow they'd drawn closer to each other, and his hand now brushed her shoulder. His heart thudded from her nearness, and his body seemed to vibrate with electricity.

"I... thought I was too..." he replied.

Now that he had met Kate, he could never return to his ordinary life. Whether he stayed with her or not, Coleman knew. He was forever changed.

And with that thought heating his blood, he leaned in, mesmerized by her lips, her sweet face.

Before either thought better of it, they kissed.

CHAPTER
SEVEN

"THAT'S THE POLE GUY OUT THERE, PUTTING THEM IN?" Jaylen asked the next morning. He gazed out the window while eating a bowl of cereal. The child insisted he preferred cereal every day rather than a hot cooked breakfast, which was the only reason Kat sat beside him with her oatmeal instead of cooking up a storm.

"Yep, that's Hayes. He works with Coleman. The poles need a day to set, so we can start working on the dock tomorrow," Kat replied.

"Is Coleman out there helping Hayes?"

"No. He was out there with him for a bit, pointing out where he wanted the poles. Then he disappeared. I don't know what he's doing."

"I bet we'll find out this afternoon." Jaylen's face

filled with such innocent and child-like mischief, Kate's heart lifted.

She laughed. "Yeah, you're right. He's probably planning some grand outdoorsman adventure for us."

She was pleased that Jaylen didn't seem too affected by the previous night's activities. When they finally sat to watch TV, she asked, "Do you remember everything that happened last night?"

"Not what the nightmare was. Only being a bobcat and feeling kind of confused. I don't know how I turned back into a boy in my sleep. Weird, right?"

"It's definitely not the norm," Kat agreed.

Jaylen settled on a Batman cartoon and shouted, "Hey, we should watch this! I didn't think of it till now, but Coleman is a lot like Batman. Isn't he?"

"How so?" Kat asked. She wasn't all that familiar with the superhero, and she wondered why Jaylen found the two men similar.

"Well, he's all quiet and brooding, for one."

"Brooding?" Kat chuckled. That was hardly a usual word for a ten-year-old.

"Yeah. They call him that all the time on the show. You know, he's like all big and strong and looks unfriendly. Probably because of something that he's thinking about that's bothering him. Not because he hates everyone around him or anything."

"Huh." Kat nodded. "That is a pretty good description for Coleman."

"And, of course, the whole kicking bad-guy butt thing."

When Kat raised an eyebrow, Jaylen immediately picked up on her distaste for violence. "I mean... Not that I've seen Coleman beat anyone up. Just that he's teaching us all those badass things like archery and fishing. I bet Batman fishes when he's vacationing." Jaylen laughed at the hilarious image.

They silently watched the rest of the episode. When the show ended, Jaylen gave her a serious look. "Coleman's parents are dead like Batman's... and mine."

Kat nodded gravely. "Coleman told you?"

He shrugged. "I guess he wanted me to know I'm not the only orphan. I have Coleman and Batman."

"You do."

"Maybe when I grow up, I'll keep other people safe like they do."

Kat was conflicted. On the one hand, she liked seeing the positive influence Coleman had on Jaylen. On the other, she didn't want Jaylen to glorify such a stoic and possibly lonely existence, like the ones

Batman and seemingly Coleman led. She didn't want that kind of life for Jaylen. She wanted him to have the warmth of family and the belonging of community, and to grow up not feeling alone.

She hoped Oren would take care of that by finding Jaylen a good family.

As Kat prepared sandwiches for lunch, she looked out the window just in time to see Coleman strolling through the backyard. He walked with purpose, his shirt off and a sledgehammer resting over his shoulder. His rippling muscles shone with sweat, and his skin was dirty, grimy.

Damn. That was a sexy surprise.

Coleman stopped to talk to Hayes and wiped his forehead with the shirt bundled in his hand. He pointed toward the house, and Kat assumed he was inviting Hayes to lunch. She'd already anticipated that, making plenty of sandwiches for everyone.

"What have you been up to all morning?" Kat asked when Coleman entered the cabin, followed by Hayes.

"Wouldn't you like to know?" Coleman's eyes sparkled with his teasing tone. Kat tilted her head to the side, assessing the man.

She'd never seen him so happy, giddy almost. Was it all the manual labor? Sweating it out with the sledgehammer cracked away some of his hard shell to let out some of his happiness. She wondered how long it would last.

It didn't take long for Kat to get her answer. Coleman showered, and just like that, his high spirits went down the drain. When he joined them, he was back to his usual grim self.

He ate quickly and then announced, "Alright, it's time to go."

Kat had imagined some spectacular surprise when Coleman walked in all happy and proud. That idea was dashed when he led them through the woods to a clearing, where he revealed his grand project.

A large pen. An eyesore, for sure, with wooden poles staked into the ground in a big circle and something like chicken wire stretched out around it.

Coleman peeled a part of the chicken wire back like he was opening the door to a candy store. He motioned Jaylen and Kat inside.

"Uhh... What is this, Coleman?" Jaylen asked, as bewildered as Kat felt.

"I call this the gladiator ring," Coleman proudly claimed.

"Ambitious," Kat said.

He shot her a look. "Jaylen, you remember what

happened last night?”

“I don’t remember my nightmare or shifting, but I remember you guys coming in. That’s when I realized I was a cat.”

“Well, it’s time you give it a try. For you to call on your cat, on purpose, so the shift doesn’t come up and surprise you anymore. You need to connect with your cat, and you might as well be intentional about it.”

Kat’s limbs were numb with cold and fear. “Wait, what? I need to talk to you.”

Coleman waved her off. “Okay, Jaylen. Now, you can take your clothes off first if you want, but it’s a little chilly today. You might get cold. If you shift in your clothes right now, it’s not a big deal. Your bobcat won’t rip up your clothes.”

Jaylen shook his head. The poor kid had probably never thought a thing about shifting and ripping clothes. “Okay, so I’ll keep my clothes on.”

“Alright. Now close your eyes and think about bobcats. What they look like, how they move, what it might feel like to be one.”

As Jaylen did so, Kat pulled Coleman by the arm to the furthest point away from him. “We hadn’t decided on a plan. Why do you have us in a pen, like farm animals? What is your endgame here?”

"I thought we had decided," Coleman replied, shocked. "He needs to practice shifting. I had Hayes bring up the posts and the wire this morning with the stuff for the dock. I figured we had to contain the bobcat if he manages to shift."

"Are you sure you weren't thinking that you might have to scare the bobcat out, and that's why you're worried we'll need to contain him?"

Coleman shrugged. "He can't be coddled. We live in a rough shifter world and have to be ready for it. If he controls his shifts, he can help himself. If he can get used to shifting, he can start to keep his wits about him and be less of a danger to himself and others around him. He has to be present with the bobcat for that to happen."

"But do we have to do that *now*? He could shift back into a bobcat and be in that terrorized state again."

"He'll get used to it."

"And what are you going to do if he shifts and gets stuck like that?"

"Same thing I did last time. It ended with me getting to be in bed with you, didn't it?" He smiled cockily at her. She hated her body's powerful reaction to him. She couldn't melt. She was trying to be stern with him.

Kat pressed her lips together and shook her head, annoyed. "There are other ways to do that, you know?"

"Yeah. I do because we talked about it last night. We'll try it slow and stuff first. If that works? Great. If not..."

Kat was about to drill into him some more. She wanted Coleman to promise he wouldn't scare Jaylen, but her attention was caught by the boy.

"Guys?" Jaylen called out, uncertain. "I think I can feel some fur trying to come out, but it's like..." He dropped off and scratched his arm. "It's just under there.".

"That's good, though, Jaylen!" Coleman said, jogging back over to his side. "How about this? You keep that feeling there, and Kat and I are going to shift. Watch us, and maybe that will help your body follow along. I think that's what helped me back in the day."

Kat followed Coleman's lead, shifting in and out of their animals a few times. When she thought they were about to shift to humans again, Coleman's bear surprised her. With a gruff roar, he tackled her to the ground.

She hissed, swatted at his face, and quickly scrambled out from underneath him to sprint away.

The round pen was only about fifty feet in diameter. Kat didn't have much distance to work with. Luckily, she was far more agile than the bear. He tried to cut across the ring, but she easily juked and got around him.

She was so focused on thwarting the bear that she almost didn't notice a little bobcat blocking her path.

Startled by the sight of him, she faltered, and the bear pinned her again.

The bobcat, bouncing around like his legs were springs, pounced first on Kat, bonking her in the head. Then he lunged for the bear, though no matter how many times Jaylen made impact, the bear didn't budge.

The bobcat growled and took a big bite of bear flank.

The bear, clearly unaffected by teeny tiny claws and teeth, swatted at the kitten.

It was all the distraction Kat needed to wriggle her way out and dart away.

Now it was two cats against one bear, and while no one was looking to do any harm, the cats sure had a good time chasing the bear and striking at him from all sides.

Finally, Coleman gave up and took a seat, his

back against one of the fence poles so he could swipe at any feline who dared come close.

Kat sat in the middle of the pen and started to groom herself. It was customary to groom and then nap after a job well done.

Jaylen copied her—the grooming part, anyway.

Kat exchanged a look with Coleman.

Now was the moment of truth.

As if in synch, both adult animals turned back into humans, watching the bobcat while they collected their clothes.

To Kat's immense relief, Jaylen transformed back into a boy only moments later.

"Holy cow! I did it." Jaylen cried, catching the clothes Coleman tossed at him. "I want to try again!"

"Let's wait on that one, buddy," Coleman said.

"It takes a lot out of you when you first shift," Kat added. "A lot of energy, that is. Besides, look how late it is. The sun is starting to set. We need to go eat and then rest." She didn't add that the boy would likely be asleep right after dinner. Shifting and then all that running was absolutely going to wear him out.

CHAPTER

EIGHT

Coleman offered to carry Jaylen back to the cabin, but the boy was stubborn. He could barely keep his eyes open while Kat prepared dinner, and Coleman had to keep nudging him to encourage him to eat his dinner.

Somehow he managed to shower and dress in his pajamas before they all curled up on the couch to watch a movie.

Jaylen was out cold in the first five minutes.

Coleman waited until the movie was over to see if Jaylen would wake up. He didn't. Not even when Coleman carried him upstairs and tucked him in his bed.

When Coleman returned downstairs, Kat was no longer sitting on the couch. He spotted her out on the back porch through the kitchen window and joined her.

"Chilly out here," he commented.

"You could build a fire," she suggested without looking at him.

He couldn't tell if that was some kind of romantic invitation, but instead of questioning it, he got right to work.

Kat sat in one of the Adirondack chairs around the firepit, and Coleman soon took the chair next to her.

"Today was fun," Kat remarked the moment he settled.

He grunted in reply.

"What? Two cats too much for you?" she teased, nudging him with her elbow.

He caught her arm, sliding his fingers down her forearm to capture her hand in his.

Slowly, he interlaced their fingers, rubbing his thumb on her silky smooth wrist, staring only at their hands while he did it. He didn't dare look up to meet her eyes.

How could he? He wasn't a romantic guy, and he certainly never felt such desire to simply hold a woman's hand before. To just touch her, to make a connection that quietly said, *we're here, in this thing, together.*

That's exactly what holding her meant to him. He wanted to stay just like this. To feel the ease of their connection. To feel the reassurance in her presence.

"Stars are sure pretty out here," she spoke softly, breaking into his thoughts.

He released his stare to finally look up at her. He wanted to see those beautiful blue eyes that glittered more than all the stars above them. She studied the twinkling night sky with such focus he was nearly jealous that it could captivate her attention so completely.

He had to be content with memorizing her moon-bathed profile. The soft curve of her cheek, the slope of her nose, her pillowy lips, her elegant throat. During the time together, he stole glances every chance he could, but he'd yet to tire of her from every angle.

"They're probably mostly satellites," he grumbled.

Nice mood-breaker, stupid, he told himself.

Luckily, she didn't pull her hand away from his or even toss a glare his way. "They're sparkly and pretty. Besides, as long as you can find the constellations, you know that you're looking at real stars up there."

"Yeah." he begrudgingly admitted, halfway afraid to look up now.

She pointed out Boötes and Virgo, and then, of course, the cat, Leo, finally landing on Ursa Major, the great bear of the sky.

He liked hearing her talk, but something about that vast expanse of space made him feel so magnificently insignificant. He realized how lucky he was to be with his fated mate.

"It's hard not to look up there without thinking that there really must be some higher power involved." Kat mused, her thoughts in sync with him once again.

"Involved in what?" he asked, testing whether or not she was really thinking the same thing as him.

She was.

"How would anyone find their mate if something like fate didn't demand it?" Kat finally turned her head away from the sky, meeting his eye before looking down at their hands and giving him a squeeze.

"More like Esme Baer," he countered.

Kat grinned at him, no longer buying into his cynical grumpiness. "Don't you think that fate works with what it has? That fate has given Esme the gift to put so many couples together?"

"That would make sense." Coleman adjusted his position in his chair, so he could lean over, closer to Kat. He felt magnetized, pulled toward her, needing to move in, needing to be nearer.

Kat copied him, and soon their foreheads touched. For a moment, they just breathed in each other's scent before he dipped his head and kissed her.

The arms of their chairs prevented him from crushing her against him, but didn't stop them from fully tasting each other, fully immersing themselves in the essence of each other. His body reveled in her touch, and his hands luxuriated in the feel of her skin and hair.

When they finally broke for air, she pulled away, standing. "I should go in," she breathed, and he could almost hear how fast and hard her heart thudded in her chest.

If she really wanted to go, she would have gone, he reasoned, and he took the opportunity to reach for her hand and tug her until she tumbled into his lap.

He caught her, his arms going around her waist as her arms were going around his neck. Their mouths met again, their kiss heated by their new and exciting exploration.

Touching, teasing.

The build-up was nearly unbearable.

He wanted to pick her up and lay them back down on the grass near the firepit. He wanted to take her and claim her right there.

But there was a kid to think about.

He forced himself to pull away, focusing his eyes on the cabin so he could do what needed to be done. "Sorry about that. You were right. You should go in before..."

"Yeah. Before," Kat said, stood and straightened her top. "I'll see you tomorrow."

By the light of the fire, he could see her lips were swollen from their kisses, and her slight smile told him she felt the same he did. *That was damn good. Too bad we can't do more.*

AFTER A COLD SHOWER and a night of tossing and turning, Coleman was up at the crack of dawn to check on the poles and get all the tools set up. He had a deck to build.

He didn't expect Jaylen and Kat to join him a few hours later.

"Can we help?" Jaylen asked. "I thought we were doing this together?"

"Uh, I was just getting stuff ready," Coleman replied. "Isn't this your video game time?"

Jaylen looked to Kat, and Coleman realized that while he hadn't meant to sound like he was rejecting the kid, he had.

"Just because it's video game time," Kat pointed out. "Doesn't mean he can't skip it and come out here to help if he wants to."

Coleman lifted an eyebrow. "You want to do this *instead* of your games?" He wasn't sure he'd understood correctly.

Jaylen nodded. "I mean, I'd say maybe practice shifting again, but it made me so tired that I don't think I'd be able to build a dock. So, yeah. I'd like to do this."

"Alright." Coleman smiled, feeling goofy for how good it felt to have the kid taking an interest in outside stuff. Or maybe because he was taking an interest in something Coleman really enjoyed. "Well, we have our wood here for the cedar decking, some brackets, corner irons, bolt kits—"

"Why are those sections done already?" Kat

pointed. "Those big squares of planks. They're already put-together?"

"Well, we could have done it all from scratch, but this is just the dock kit. It comes with those prefab sections that we just have to connect to the poles out in the water."

"So then, what are we building?" Jaylen asked.

Coleman laughed. "We'll need to reinforce all the corners, place the brackets and then attach them to the poles out there. That's going to be plenty. First, we'll build the dock section that's attached to the shore."

He showed Jaylen the power tools and gave safety tips for using them before they started working on the deck.

"I didn't notice that Hayes put these in yesterday," Kat commented, pointing at the base planks.

"Believe me, you're going to be glad some work was done ahead of time," Coleman warned.

An hour in, she told him he was right.

It was a *lot* of work.

By the time noon rolled around, they had made progress, almost having all of the shore section completed.

"Come in for lunch," Kat said, but Coleman refused. He was in the zone.

Jaylen stayed with him, and Kat allowed it while she went in to prepare something.

When she finally returned, the bounty enticed them away from their work.

"You won't have the strength to work for much longer if you don't break for food," she lectured. "Now, go wash up."

Coleman showed Jaylen to the garden hose, and they both rinsed off, using some rags to clean the sweat and dirt from their faces.

Satisfied, Kat laid a blanket out on the hill between the cabin and the pond and set out the array of food.

Coleman's stomach rumbled. "How did you do all this?"

"Thinking ahead." Kat laughed. "I had Gia drop off some groceries while we were out there. We have fish cakes from the leftover trout, and I also made some salmon cakes with fish Gia brought up. I figured they would pair well with these zucchini fritters with Greek yogurt dip. There's sweet coleslaw and pickled mango."

It was all Coleman could do, not tell her right then and there, *I love you.*

CHAPTER

NINE

AS THEY MUNCHED AWAY ON THEIR PICNIC, KAT WAS entranced by Coleman. He seemed so different to her. The usual protective coldness that he'd shown at first was completely gone, and she couldn't help but think that the person she was looking at was the *real* Coleman. The man who hides beneath the tough outer shell.

All while working that morning, he smiled and nodded enthusiastically while Jaylen asked questions and used the tools. Every time he bumped the boy with his elbow and said *good job*, Kat's heart swelled.

This is who Coleman should be all the time, Kat thought. *Not that hard shell guy.*

She cleaned up after they finished eating and

came back just in time to see the prefab pieces going on the poles.

Coleman's clothes were in a pile along the shore, and she got a great view of his torso as he held up the large prefab square over his head.

"Can I help?" she called as Coleman walked the heavy loaf to the first set of poles

"Nah," Coleman shouted back. "The kid's got this. You just sit there and look pretty."

She heard Coleman speak to Jaylen, "Don't ever say that to a woman for real, okay? I'm only teasing Kat, and she knows it."

"Cause you like her," Jaylen replied.

Coleman's eyes flicked up to the boy. "Why would you say that?"

Kat imagined he probably rolled his eyes before telling Coleman, "Dude, if it's so obvious that a ten-year-old can see it, then you probably shouldn't try to deny it."

"Hand me that joint," Coleman said, clearly deciding to ignore him.

He and Jaylen worked on attaching the sections of the deck. The boy handed him the joints and bolts to secure the dock to the poles.

When Coleman came back to shore, Kat looked

away. She didn't want to ogle him while a child was present.

When he walked back out to the next set of poles with the prefab piece above her head, she couldn't help but think that he looked picture-perfect. A man made of muscles, dripping wet, smiling as he instructed Jaylen.

They cheered and high-fived after completing the dock, and Kat braved the first walk all the way to the edge. She was surprised by its sturdiness.

"Come on. Let's grab our rods from the shed," Coleman said, his face lit up like a kid's on Christmas. "It's dusk which is a great time for fish. It will be dark fast, so it's now or wait for tomorrow!"

Jaylen and Coleman ran off, leaving Kat on the dock alone.

With the sun setting and the excited chatter of the two males behind her, she looked out at the peaceful ripples of the pond.

This feels like paradise.

A moment later, paradise turned to chaos as they returned with all the fishing accouterments.

"This is *much better* than a bouncy boat," Kat assured them while they fished. "You all did a good job."

"You helped too," Jaylen pointed out. "So *we all* did a good job."

They caught a few fish—to properly break in the dock on its first day—and then called it. The sweaty guys each took showers, and Kat worked on getting dinner together.

Afterward, Jaylen asked if they could do a campfire again, specifically so they could sit out back and admire the view of the dock.

Of course they couldn't refuse him. The pride he held for the dock was something Kat hadn't seen coming, but she thought back to Coleman's assessment on their first full day together, when he'd created the first training circuit for Jaylen.

He'd said that the outdoorsy activities would build Jaylen's confidence, and Coleman was right.

Jaylen helped Coleman make the fire, and even though Jaylen had played no video games or watched any television that day, he happily sat outside and talked with them until he started to nod off.

Once alone, Coleman and Kat sat around the fire in silence. Coleman checked the security app on his phone. Not only did it have different camera views from all around the outside of the house, but there were some in the halls too, which would alert them of any strange activity while they were outside.

"That dock really is nice," Kat broke the silence.

"I know what you're going to say," Coleman started.

"What?" Kat asked, confused. She hadn't been about to say anything in particular.

"That the kid needs to be a kid. That letting him make a dock today was better than trying to spend every day training."

"I didn't say that. Not that I agree with the sentiment, but are *you* saying maybe *you* think it?" Kat smiled a bit smugly.

"Maybe," Coleman grumbled.

"The only thing I'd thought at all was that you were right about him doing outdoorsy stuff building his confidence. He had a blast."

"You think so?" Coleman turned his head to look for her with such an earnest expression that she realized he hadn't known whether or not he was doing good for the kid.

"Oh my God, Coleman, yeah! Everything you've done has been great. And honestly, the kid thinks you're a superhero."

"He told you that?"

"Yeah, he says you're like Batman."

He laughed, shaking his head. "A vigilante. That fits."

"Not exactly what he said, but sure, I guess."

His phone chimed, and he pulled it out. He quickly typed a text before shoving the device back into his pocket. He rolled his shoulders, and his whole demeanor changed.

"You seem more relaxed than usual, and it's more than just the fun of building a dock. What's up with you?"

Coleman shrugged. "I feel like this is coming to an end soon. It's been long enough."

"Do you know something I don't?" Kat asked, wondering what was in the texts that had perked him up.

He walked over to her chair and pulled her to her feet and into his arms. "Right now, all I want is to think about you."

That was certainly a change. Previously he wanted to ignore their mutual attraction to focus on work. Now, his guard was down, and Kat felt the full force of his attention on her alone.

"All you wanna think about is me?"

"Yeah," he whispered. "I told you I didn't want to think about you... me... us. But it's been in my thoughts since the moment I met you."

"It has?"

"I had to do my job and tried to ignore my attraction, but that's impossible. Not with you here. So beautiful. So good with the kid. I've wanted to pull you in my arms every moment of every day. I've wanted to do this."

She tilted her head up, and as soon as she parted her lips, his mouth was crushing hers, claiming hers. She melted into him.

"You think we can sneak inside?" he asked when they came up for air.

"We just have to be very quiet," Kat replied.

"If it means I can be with you, I can do it."

COLEMAN WOKE to a text from Oren.

Plan is in motion. Target heading your way. Team is tracking him but should be in range in about thirty minutes.

Coleman replied, *On it*, then snuck from the bed.

Oren's network had leaked their location to lure out the killer. It had worked. Roderick Voris, the man who'd tried to prove himself to the Santibanez pack—the rival wolf pack to Oren's bear clan—was now on his way to the cabin. His sole purpose was to tie up loose ends.

Coleman would never let Roderick Voris have the chance to hurt Jaylen again.

He cast a glance at Kat, who was still sleeping soundly. She was absolutely beautiful, from her wavy blonde hair to her round happy face to the exquisite curves.

Would she still look at *him* the same after he did what he needed to today?

He couldn't think about it. He had a job to do.

Coleman wouldn't just do it because Oren ordered it. He'd do it because the kid needed it. Jaylen needed to know he was safe. That he wouldn't have to look over his shoulder for the rest of his life. That the man who killed his parents had been taken out.

CHAPTER

TEN

Kat woke up to an empty bed.

Though it wasn't unexpected since Coleman got up and going before she and Jaylen did, she was disappointed. She'd hoped to wake up and immediately feel his arms around her, his chin against her head.

Sighing, she left the bed, showered, and dressed.

When she entered the kitchen, she looked around. Coleman was nowhere to be found in the cabin or outside.

Maybe he's setting up another gladiator ring or something like it, she mused. If that were the case, though, why wouldn't he have wanted to stay in bed with her instead?

Because his priority is Jaylen, she chided herself.

She knew Coleman felt strongly for her, and it was far too early to start worrying about things between them. *I'm sure he just woke up and immediately felt guilty for indulging last night, so he got to work preparing stuff for Jaylen.*

She began to make her oatmeal when she heard Jaylen's door open, followed by his clunky footsteps down the stairs.

"Morning, Kat," he said. "Where's Coleman?"

"I don't know. Haven't seen him," Kat replied.

Jaylen sat next to her at the kitchen island and ate his cereal. They both faced the back, where they could see the pond off in the distance.

"So cool we made that, huh?" Jaylen commented when he got up to rinse out his cereal bowl. "Oh, hey! There's Coleman. There's someone with him."

Kat thought maybe it was Hayes, helping out with whatever project Coleman had going on for the day.

"Coleman has a gun!" Jaylen cried, and Kat snapped her head up.

"What?" She flew to the back door just in time to see Coleman throw the other man to the ground, holding a gun to his head.

"Jaylen, get out here," Coleman shouted.

Kat ran out first. "What are you doing?"

She caught Jaylen and held him back from running too close to Coleman.

"Jaylen, does this man look familiar to you?" Coleman asked.

As Kat held him, she felt Jaylen's whole body start to shake.

"Jaylen, answer. I know you don't remember that night, but there's a piece of you that *does* know. So look at this guy and tell me: is this the man who killed your parents?"

Jaylen nodded his head. Kat starred in absolute horror. "Why are you doing this?" she cried. He was forcing Jaylen to relive the trauma. And for what?

Coleman ignored her. "What do you want to say to him, Jaylen? Say it now because you won't get another chance." Kat heard a click signaling Coleman was getting ready to shoot.

She couldn't believe it.

In front of her was a man Kat had never seen— and not the stranger on the ground. The man standing above him was a stone-cold killer. Coleman wasn't posturing. He had every intention of following through with it.

How could that be? How could this man be the same one who'd smiled so much while they built the dock yesterday? How could he be the man who'd gone out of his way to make a gladiator ring to train Jaylen to shift?

How could he be the man who made love to her last night?

It didn't make any sense.

This wasn't the *real* Coleman.

He was only doing this because he had the misguided idea that shooting the murderer would be good for Jaylen. That doing this would *help* Jaylen. That's all Coleman really wanted to do— help the boy.

Kat knew that Colman *thought* this was who he needed to be, and he would follow through with it. But it wasn't the man he really was. The *real* Coleman wouldn't go out of his way to commit violence.

Which meant she could stop this. She could get through to him.

"What are you doing?" She tugged Jaylen a bit further back. "This isn't civilized! You're going to shoot this man in front of Jaylen?"

She moved to take Jaylen into the house, and Coleman yelled for her to stop. "He needs to see this. He needs to see the killer of his parents taken out. That way, he'll know justice was served."

"This isn't justice!" Kat cried. "This is violence

on top of violence. It doesn't have to be that way."

"You said yesterday I was right about what he needed."

"That is totally different! You're *not* right now!" Kat tried desperately to make eye contact, knowing if she could just snap him out of it, he'd change his mind. Coleman was laser-focused on the other man, a world away from her.

"You don't understand. You haven't been in our shoes. Not knowing if you're ever safe or not," Coleman replied. "But with this trash dead, Jaylen can sleep at night. He doesn't have to grow up thinking he needs to keep an eye out. You can't speak for what's right or wrong in this situation when you've never lived it."

He was speaking from experience. He had lived his whole life fearing the person who killed his father would be back for him.

But that didn't matter because she *knew* that witnessing a murder wouldn't help Jaylen in any way.

"Everything you've done for Jaylen has been about you wanting him *not* to grow up the same way you did," Kat said calmly, hoping her words would get through to him while the strange man cowered on the ground. "Maybe this is what you wanted, what you needed, but it's not what's going to help Jaylen find a different path than you did."

If you kill someone in front of him, he's going to think that's the right way to live.

"Jaylen, speak your peace," Coleman ordered, still ignoring Kat.

At least, on the surface, it seemed he was ignoring her, but she had a feeling she was needling her way in.

In the same soft tone, she continued. "Don't let the rage left over from your childhood get the better of you. You don't want Jaylen to live like that. You want him to be free of lifelong torment, right? Then show him the *right* path to justice."

"Take him to jail," Jaylen said, speaking for the first time.

At the sound of his voice, Coleman finally looked in their direction, his eyes first landing on Jaylen and then going to Kat.

She shook her head, silently pleading for him not to shoot the man.

"Fine."

Coleman shoved the man to the ground and held him down by pressing a knee to his back while he pulled out his phone.

Jaylen struggled in Kat's grasp, trying to run to

Coleman, but Kat dragged him back toward the cabin.

The boy didn't protest.

She stalked into the house, pulling out her phone to call Gia. She wanted a ride out of there and fast. To her surprise, the woman was already waiting inside.

"I didn't hear you drive up," Kat said.

"A lot was going on outside." Gia shrugged, though Kat could see the concern in the other woman's eyes.

Kat nodded. "I need you to take us back to Idlewyld."

"That's why I'm here. I placed a suitcase in your room, Jaylen. You can pack up whatever you want to take with you, and we'll head out of here."

"What about Coleman? Is he coming too?" Jaylen looked toward the back door.

Gia shook her head. "He's got some business with Hayes."

"And where am I going?" Jaylen asked.

Kat wanted to know the same thing.

"You're going to stay with Oren for a few days, and then you'll be going to your new home."

Jaylen looked up at Kat, and his big soft brown eyes broke her heart. "I…"

She could imagine what he wanted to say. He wanted to stay with her and Coleman. But that wasn't possible. "It's going to be fine," Kat vowed. "Oren is a good man, and I guarantee you he's found some great people to take care of you. Coleman and I will still be your friends, though. We'll still see you. We'll visit."

"Promise?"

"Absolutely."

Gia helped Jaylen pack while Kat pulled her own things together. Her room had a view of the backyard, and she watched Coleman and Hayes haul Roderick off. Yeah, it was much better than being dead, but she was still bitter about it.

I can't be with a man who thinks it's okay to shoot someone in front of a kid, no matter the reason.

I can't be with a man who does that kind of thing for a living.

I'm a nurse. I save lives. Whatever he is... he destroys them.

Those two kinds of people can never be together.

She was full of sadness. Sadness at saying goodbye to Jaylen and sadness at the fact that Coleman was her fated mate—the only one she'd ever have—and yet he was a man she could never be with.

CHAPTER

ELEVEN

The two full weeks of her leave weren't up yet, so Kat grew bored, sitting at home for the next few days. She even tried to go back to work early, and they told her no. Union rules forbade it, or so she was told.

Her apartment was too quiet. She couldn't find anything to do. No binge-worthy shows could keep her attention, no books, either. She even went out and tried buying crafts she'd done as a kid—knitting, painting, and cross-stitch. None of it worked.

All she could think about was fishing on the dock with her boys.

What was Jaylen doing now? Had he met his new family yet? Could she keep in touch or get updates about him?

Kat always cared about her patients, but something about Jaylen was much more personal, and she couldn't stop missing him.

She considered calling Oren for an update, but every time she thought about it, she was overcome with disgust. Oren was Coleman's boss. Undoubtedly Oren was the reason Coleman had a gun to that man's head.

So she didn't call.

Thinking about Oren and Coleman's relationship—knowing that Oren had taken Coleman in and given him a job when he was young and impressionable—made her think back to her clowder. How lucky had she been to grow up with responsible adults who provided good examples of role models?

For so long, she'd been glad to go off on her own, to discover who she was outside of her community. Now, after her time with Jaylen and Coleman, she suddenly missed home badly. What she wouldn't give for a good old clowder barbeque, complete with tons of kids running around.

Bored, annoyed, and haunted by regret, Kat decided she had to get out of her house. But for what? And where would she go?

She tried calling Nila but got no answer.

She could go out to dinner by herself, but she had already eaten.

She wracked her brain for what she used to do before becoming a nurse.

She used to go out clubbing when she was in college. A lot. It had been her favorite pastime. Drinking too much, forgetting every lousy grade, every lonely minute, and any other bad thing that had happened that day or that week. Meeting guys who had one thing on their mind and were ready to worship her for a night. Maybe returning to clubbing could help her find someone that would make her forget Coleman.

Highly unlikely, her common sense said, but her mind was made up.

Kat had buried her old, fun-loving self in responsibility. She hadn't realized it before, but she knew it now. She became that party girl because she was disappointed when she got to the real world and missed her family so much. And then she became a workaholic, so she never slowed down enough to feel the pain that had never gone away.

But her time with Coleman and Jaylen had let her feel like her *original* self. Not party girl or workaholic, but just chill, *happy* Kat.

This is too much thinking, she decided, realizing her thoughts were spiraling.

Se put on the closest thing she had to party clothes—a sequin top and a pair of black leggings—and headed to the one shifter club she knew of downtown. The one place that served the special kind of alcohol that could actually let a shifter get tipsy—even though it didn't last very long.

Wait, there is one friend who's always up for a good time!

She called up Mikel, and they met up at a club. Mikel wasn't living in Idlewyld, but it didn't take him long to get there. By the time he arrived, Kat was already many shots in, letting loose on the dance floor.

"Kudos on the hot guys," Mikel said. "But perhaps you should take a break from all this for a bit. Maybe we can get some nachos, sit down at a booth..."

"Why?" Kat snapped. "What *exactly* has *not* being a party girl gotten me?"

Mikel blinked. "I've never seen you like this."

"Cause we haven't known each other that long. If you were Nila—who, by the way, *did know me but didn't answer her phone!*—then you would have been, like... *known* me that way before."

She knew she was slurring and mixing up her words. She also knew that if she knew she was slurring, she could probably snap herself out of it. Act a little more rational. A little more mature. Stable. Whatever.

She didn't want any of that. Because that meant thoughts of Coleman and how in those *stupid* days together, she'd started to get comfortable. Some foolish part of her had made the laughable mistake of believing that she might actually end up with her fated mate.

And now she had to deal with the truth. He was a bad man, and no matter how much she wanted him, no matter how much she missed him, she could never allow herself to see him again.

"Come on, come on, we're going to sit. I haven't seen you in forever, and I want to catch up." Mikel tugged her off the dance floor.

She thought about refusing, but her mouth was dry, and she really could use a drink. Plus, she thought he mentioned something about nachos, which sounded good...

Mikel settled her in a booth and went off on a search for a waitress and nachos. Kat watched as he pulled out his phone. That wouldn't bring them nachos any sooner. Who was he calling, anyway? A nacho genie? Nope. It was Probably Nila.

"Kat?" Her head snapped around to the owner of the voice.

"Coleman? What the hell are you doing here?" The vision of him instantly sobered her up. Her body flushed, her heart started beating rapidly, and immediately, she remembered how strongly she felt for him.

For his part, Coleman seemed unaffected by her presence. He casually shrugged. "You doing okay?"

She starred at him with her mouth agape, in disbelief at his casual attitude.

Luckily, Mikel returned to their booth just then. "Hello, have we met? I'm Mikel."

"Coleman."

"Ah, Coleman, how nice to meet you. Are you friends with Kat, or are you just some man trying to pick up someone for the night?" Mikel made a sour face, showing that he thought it was likely the latter.

"A friend. I was just going," Coleman mumbled, shoving his hands in his pockets. He walked away with just one last glance at Kat.

Mikel looked from Coleman's back to Kat. "Don't

tell me that handsome man is why you're out here in a tailspin."

"Why?" Kat asked, taking a sip from one of the water glasses the waitress dropped off at the table.

"Because with the way he looked at you, it's obvious he'd do anything for you. What happened? He cheated, and you refuse to forgive?"

She shook her head. A different waitress came by with the gigantic plate of nachos, and she readily dug in. "It's just star-crossed, you know? Never meant to be, and then stupid fate put in both our heads to come here tonight? Why, Mikel? Why does fate want us to run into each other when it's *obviously* not going to work?"

"I'd say because your definition of *obviously* is a bit off."

"No, believe me. I'm not going to get into it because I don't want to be a blabbermouth that ends up sleeping with the *fishes*, but I assure you, it won't work."

The conversation turned to other subjects, and as the plate of nachos disappeared and the night wore down, Kat could only think about how she hoped that her feelings toward Coleman would fade, though she wasn't sure it was possible.

"Hey, look who the cat dragged in!" Mikel said, pointing at a woman approaching their table.

"I see you got ahold of Nila," Kat sighed.

"Well, someone had to drive you home," he replied. "It was nice seeing you. Hopefully, next time will be a bit better. Ciao!"

Nila's mate Pryce had dropped her off at the club, and then Nila drove Kat's car to take them back to her apartment.

The next morning, Kat awoke to find Nila had already run out and picked up some delicious hang-over food—tacos from the best local Mexican food truck.

"I'm sorry I didn't call you back," Nila said once they dug into their food.

"And you thought that breakfast tacos would make me forgive you?" Kat asked before smiling at her friend. "Cause if so, you were right."

"So, I guess I can just assume the cabin trip wasn't good?"

Kat growled and took a sip of coffee.

"That bad? Really? I thought, with Esme involved..."

"You thought she was setting me up with my fated mate?" Kat finally found her words. "Well, you weren't wrong."

"But things didn't go well?"

Kat sighed and added salsa to her next taco. "They did for a while. But it all ended badly."

"I'm sorry to hear that," Nila replied. After a moment, she added, "Oren and Anya want you to come for dinner tonight. To thank you."

"I don't think so. Thanks, though." Kat shrugged and focused on the egg and bacon delicacy in front of her.

"It's a sendoff for Jaylen."

Kat turned back to Nila, raising her eyebrows. "Will his new family be there? I'd like to meet them. I think it would give me some peace of mind."

Nila nodded. "I bet it would. I don't know who all is going to be there, though."

"Coleman, no doubt," Kat muttered.

"Yes, but you shouldn't let that stop you," Nila cautioned. "You'll regret it if you don't say a final goodbye to Jaylen."

"It's not a final goodbye. I told him we'd stay in touch."

"Sure, you said that, but will it really happen? Or

will you bury yourself in work and then suddenly look up, and five years have passed?"

"I don't know." Kat sighed. Hearing her friend's words and knowing it was a likely scenario. "When is it better to stay in someone's life or just let yourself fade from their memories like every other horrible thing that's happened in his recent life?"

"He's asked for you," Nila said softly.

"Coleman?"

"No, Jaylen," Nila answered. A look of understanding crossed her face. "You are stuck on him, though, huh? Coleman?"

"He's my fated mate," Kat snapped. "Of course I'm affected by the situation, but that doesn't mean I'm stuck on him. I'll get over it. Things will get back to normal."

"Sure, I guess. I mean, I've seen Coleman. He doesn't look better off than you. I think they both miss you."

"Nila, do you know what they do for a living?" Kat asked, and then she thought of Nila's mate. "What.... *Pryce* does for a living, working for Oren?"

Nila wiped off her hands before turning her chair to face Kat, preparing for a serious conversation. "Yeah, I do know. And you know what else? That lifestyle isn't unfamiliar to me."

"What is that supposed to mean?"

"It means that my father was like Oren back when I was growing up. He was the leader."

"Of a *mob*?" Kat gasped.

"Something like that."

Kat's mouth dropped open in shock. "This makes no sense. Why are there shifter mobs? Why are you're talking like they're common?"

"Because it's more common than you'd think," Nila replied. "And the fact that you didn't know about it means you grew up in a way... Well, you were lucky. You didn't have to worry about rogue shifters moving in on your clowder. You didn't have to worry about violence rampant in your streets because the human authorities couldn't control the shifter gangs."

"I always knew that the shifter world hid from humans, but I thought it was mostly because humans can be dangerous towards things they don't understand. I never expected it to be the opposite. Why don't people rise up against the shifters?"

"Because shifters are stronger than humans, and when it comes down to it, the shifters would win. So people mind their own business. They leave these kinds of towns and go where else these problems don't exist. A safe place that allows them self-governance."

"And that opens them up to organized crime?"

"In a city overrun with crime, yes, and rather than the government or law enforcement controlling things poorly, the top families keep the peace."

"And you're just okay with this?"

"It's how I was raised, yeah. It's what makes sense to me. If Pryce or Oren or any of them did *bad* things, then I wouldn't be. But as long as I know there are shifters out there who want to deal drugs and arms and in human trafficking, then I'm happy that the people in charge are keeping them out."

Kat didn't know what to say. "Well... that's a lot to take in. To think about."

Nila stood. "Well, you can take your time on that, but you really need to decide if you'll say goodbye to Jaylen. I'd highly recommend that you do."

TWELVE

COLEMAN ARRIVED FOR DINNER AT THE CAVALLI'S HOME and instantly looked around for Kat.

When he saw her at the club the night before, it gutted him. He saw the torment in her eyes when he said hello to her, and he hated it.

It was almost as bad as the look in her eyes when he almost shot Roderick. It haunted him.

He was glad she'd been able to convince him not to.

And he'd been even more relieved when he'd met with Oren afterward, and his boss told him he'd done the right thing. Oren didn't care one way or another what happened to Roderick. As long as the boy knew that Roderick wasn't a free man lurking in the shadows, Oren felt the job was done.

"Coleman!" Jaylen said, running up to him.

In the few days since they returned from the cabin, he visited with the boy. He apologized for the violent scene and told Jaylen in no uncertain terms that he had been wrong. He avoided further questions—such as how many people he'd killed in the past or if he was going to give up that kind of life—and somehow managed to get them back to appropriate topics.

Jaylen even convinced Coleman to play some video games with him.

Nothing that involved shooting or guns, of course.

"Hey, kid! Looking good," Coleman greeted him, presenting a hand for a low-five hand slap.

"They say I'm going to a new family."

"That's what they tell me too."

"I thought maybe it was you. And Kat." Jaylen's eyes darkened with disappointment.

Coleman uncomfortably shoved his hands in his pockets. "Well, I'm sure whoever it is will be much better than either of us. Trust me."

Jaylen's mouth twisted in a scowl. "We'll see," he said and then walked away.

"Sometimes fatherhood is a different kind of calling," Oren lectured, walking up behind Coleman. "It's no less important than any other job."

"The kid's got a lot in common with you," Pryce appeared on Coleman's other side, as though both men had been watching him and waiting for a chance to butt in. "If you hadn't had the right kind of role models that guided you, who knows how you would have ended up."

"The kid is already far different than me," Coleman grumbled. "Putting Roderick away made sure Jaylen wouldn't grow up feeling the need for vengeance or constantly looking over his shoulder."

"You think that's what's going to happen? That —*poof*—all is right in his world?" Pryce asked.

"I have no idea," Coleman admitted. "I'd like to hope so, but yeah. The kid probably has challenges ahead of him. I know if he ends up with someone like Kat, he'll be in good hands. She had a way of making him smile, making him have fun, making him seem like a kid again."

He didn't see Kat arrive, but he finally spotted her at the dinner table. She seemed to be doing her best to avoid looking at him.

Dinner seemed to last forever, which was part torture, part self-flagellation. He tried to convince himself he could do what needed to be done.

If you're such a big strong mob guy, you can't be scared to do this. Shooting and fighting aren't strength and bravery. Approaching the woman you love and convincing her you'll do anything to make things work is.

"Kat, could we talk? Please?" he said, approaching her after everyone left the dinner table.

For a moment, he feared she would say no.

"Please?" he asked again, and she relented, nodding and following him out to the back porch.

The moment the doors closed behind them, Kat asked, "Do you deal drugs, or mess around in human trafficking? Do you harm people who don't deserve it?"

"What? God, no!" He wanted to ask how she could think that, but he surmised that seeing him hold a gun to someone's head had made an impression. A bad one that led to these kinds of questions. "No, totally no. We're in protection, that's all. We keep people safe from rogue shifters who would otherwise exploit and harm lesser shifters and humans."

"Okay," Kat said.

"In some towns, the shifters stay out of human dealings and just handle their own business, but

Idlewyld has a bad history and needs someone to be in charge."

"And money laundering, I'd guess? Since otherwise, how are you explaining your earnings?" Kat added.

He shrugged noncommittally. "You might see some poker games," Coleman admitted. "Betting on sporting events, stuff like that, but only ever with the people who can afford it. We don't prey on people with gambling addictions and then break their kneecaps when they can't pay."

"Oh. Well, that's good."

"Kat... I'm sorry."

"Sure," she shrugged. He was clearly not forgiven. "You were doing your job."

"That's not entirely true," Coleman said. "I wasn't ordered to... I mean, Oren never directly said to..."

Kat nodded. "I figured you were acting on your own behalf. I mean, the part of you that wished you could have done that to the person who'd killed *your* parents."

"I wouldn't have found peace from it, though. I know that now." He sighed and grabbed the porch railing while looking out over Oren's backyard.

"Nila kind of explained things to me." Kat took a

seat in one of the porch chairs, further away from him than he liked. She sighed deeply before continuing. "I'm not... *okay* with this kind of thing... but at least I understand it more. I... understand the need for the kind of thing you do."

"I've missed you like crazy." Coleman looked over his shoulder at her. Unwelcomed tears prickled his eyes, and a painful lump formed in his throat. "The moment you and Jaylen left the cabin, I was gutted. I tried to think of what to do, and I just didn't know where to start."

"A phone call, maybe?" she suggested.

"Would you have talked to me? You didn't at the club yesterday."

She shrugged sadly. "I don't know."

Coleman nodded, turning back toward the trees.

The door to the patio opened, and Oren sauntered out. "Hey, you two crazy kids. It's good to see you together."

"Hi, Oren," Kat greeted.

Coleman said nothing. He was busy pulling himself together, swallowing that damn throat lump.

Oren continued. "So, are you two going to work out your differences and make a home for Jaylen, or what?"

"Uh..." Kat started.

"You haven't shown her?" Oren asked Coleman.

"No..." Coleman said.

Oren sighed dramatically. "Well, get on it. There's a vulnerable young kid here who needs the two of you to sort out your differences so he can have some stability."

With that, Oren patted Coleman on the shoulder and went back into his house.

Kat shook her head toward Coleman apologetically, standing as though she were getting ready to leave. "I'm sorry. It doesn't matter how I feel about you. It doesn't matter if your mob life isn't all bad. I can't be with someone like that... someone who holds a gun to someone's head with every intention of..."

He saw that it pained her to think about it. He stepped over to her, pulled out his phone, and opened a photo album. "Here."

"What is this?"

"Files. On properties. From your hometown."

"What?" Kat took the device, looking down at it, and then back up to him, confused.

"I... I want to build a life with you and Jaylen from the ground up. I've scouted the available properties, and I've pulled together some blueprints similar to the cabin. You know, for nostalgia or familiarity or whatever. Anyway, you can modify them…"

"You looked at properties…" Kat gasped. "In my hometown? But… your job here? Your clan?"

"If your clowder of lynxes will accept a bear, I'd join for you and Jaylen in a heartbeat," Coleman said, swiping from one photo to the next, showing her all the research he'd done in the days since they'd separated. "Oren has taken good care of me, and the clan's been a great place to be, but just because we move doesn't mean we can't come back and visit. I know you'd want to visit Nila."

"You want me to quit my job and go home?" Kat asked.

"I want you to maybe look into jobs closer to your old home so that we can build a life there. So we can let Jaylen grow up in the eutopia you told me so much about."

"You'd really be able to leave this behind? Because I don't want to wake up in ten years and learn that you've been living a secret mob life…"

He took hold of both of her arms, pulling her to face him. H looked her straight in the eyes. "Kat, I would *never* do that. I never believed I was worthy of love. That the world had a plan for me that included having a stable family. But meeting my mate at the same time when I met a kid who needed someone in the same way that I'd needed someone when I was in his situation... it made me realize that I can do better."

He sighed, steadying himself before continuing. "I can have better. I can make a good life for myself and those I care about. I've never *wanted* to be in the mob. I never sought it out. It just was there. Oren took me in, and the same could happen for Jaylen.... But I won't let it. I won't have any secrets because I want better for him. And for you. For you *with* me."

Her pretty eyes fluttered in surprise.

Coleman had said all he could. He had no more words, so he did the one last thing he needed to do, hoping she'd forgive him.

He kissed her.

EPILOGUE

Moving back to the clowder was a strange feeling for Kat.

She never thought she would be back there, but the moment their new place was built and decorated, they moved in. She couldn't believe they'd ever lived anywhere else.

Their new home was on the clowder's lands, right on the lake. There were other houses all around it, and on their first day there, Jaylen made friends with the neighbor kids—three of them, all around his age.

Seeing him run around the backyard with other children gave her absolute certainty that they were where they were supposed to be.

Coleman walked up behind her and wrapped his

arms around her. Together, they watched Jaylen out the window. The perfect sight set to the sweet and loving gesture was the icing on the cake.

"So, how is your cookie-cutter, good old American *housedad* life going?" Kat asked him. She had easily found a job, but Coleman wasn't sure what to do. For now, they decided he would stay home for a bit and help Jaylen acclimate.

"Thinking about doing my own little handyman business," he replied. "See that porch next door? Clearly needs to be rebuilt. And the neighbors on the other side, they definitely need a new roof."

"Well, when people learn you basically built our place, they might insist you start a homebuilding business."

"We'll see. I'm starting with our dock, anyway. Ordered some cedar planks."

That evening Coleman asked them both to join him at the dock and surprised them with a boat. Not a little rowboat like they had at the cabin, but a nice pontoon boat that could seat many people—or sunbathing cats.

"I don't know, Coleman," Jaylen said. "Maybe you should have spent your money on a cabana 'cause that's probably as far as Kat will go in this lake."

"That's where you're wrong!" Kat said, tousling his hair before she rushed past him and onto the boat. "I'm not staying behind."

"But you hate boats!" Jaylen protested, getting on behind her and waiting while Coleman untied the boat.

Coleman walked past her on his way to the console, and Kat grabbed him by his shirt, pulling him in for a kiss.

Jaylen issued an obligatory *Ewwww,* and Kat pulled back, shaking her head. "All I know is I'd rather be with the two of you than left alone on shore."

Kat and Jaylen took a seat, and Coleman sat at the controls, driving them out on the lake.

Kat looked over the beauty of her new life, and she knew it was all right.

If the scariest thing that she experienced was a little jumping of her stomach as they race across the water, she'd take it.

The End.

ALSO BY RENEE HEWETT

FURRY UNITED COALITION NEWBIE ACADEMY

Goose and the Ocelot

Moose and the Narwhal

Zeus and the Raptor

THE NIGHTSHADE GUILD

Sunny Mage

Magic Clouded

Illuminating Time

CRIMSON MOON HIDEAWAY

Chimera's Edge

Harpy's Escape

Flame and Mist

About the Author

Renee Hewett writes paranormal romance. Before becoming a full-time writer she worked in marketing, web writing, and editing. She's volunteered for at many events, such as C4 Comic Con, Can-Con, and Romancing the Capital.

ReneeHewett.com

Facebook reader group

Sign up for Renee's Newsletter